THE GROWING YEARS

An inspirational story of success

notionpress
.com

THE GROWING YEARS

An inspirational story of success

SHABBIR SABUWALA

notionpress.com

Notion Press

5 Muthu Kalathy Street, Triplicane,

Chennai - 600 005

First Published by Notion Press 2015

ISBN: 978-93-84878-77-1

Dedication

This book is dedicated to my parents who ensured that I received sufficient education to be able to write a book someday. I also attribute to them my genetic ability to be creative.

This book is for Anagha, my wife, who has been with me through thick and thin over the last 20 years of my life.

This book is for Shirin, my daughter, who looks up to me and admires me for my knowledge and creativity.

This book is for Rachna for being a wonderful human being and the inspiration for this book.

Acknowledgment

Firstly, I have to thank Puja Lalwani – a dynamic young writer and editor. Her intensive reading and editing has tremendously helped me in completing this book successfully.

I would also like to thank Anagha, Rachna and Shirin for proofreading the book multiple times to ensure a more flawless reading experience

Preface

They say that 'Truth is stranger than fiction' and I strongly believe that! But I also believe that narrating bland facts can be boring. They need to be delicately seasoned with the flavors of drama to make it a spicy read. Hence, I preferred to author a fiction inspired from real life events. It always proves to be a much more interesting and inspirational read - an ideal blend of drama and the strange reality. Of course, one has to wait for an incident worth while writing about, before actually writing a complete book on it. In my case, it took 17 years of professional experience before I came across such an incident. But, in the meanwhile, I congregated sufficient professional knowledge for me to write a book which is not only an interesting story, but also imparts information which can transform a young designer to a successful entrepreneur.

I am Shabbir Sabuwala, a qualified architect and the Director of Dessign7 Interiors Pvt. Ltd., an interior design studio. We specialize in architectural and interior designing for residential projects. I have always been assisted in business by my lovely wife Anagha, a qualified electronics engineer. And what keeps us going is the love of our lives, our daughter Shirin, who has spent most of her growing years in Dessign7, learning from all adults around her.

Throughout my professional tenure, I have come to realize that an individual's capabilities are limited. Without intelligent help, growth in business is just not possible. Finding this help is a rarity and because of this most proprietary businesses cannot break through the glass ceiling. Fortunately for me, this help has always been extended to me firstly by my wife, who has always held my hand encouragingly and supported me throughout rough and smooth journey of life. The second intelligent help came from Rachna Vora, a ten-year younger junior, who never failed to surprise me with the immense capability she displayed from time to time. Her relationship with Dessign7 was symbiotic, where they both catapulted each other to greater heights.

I would also like to commend her parents for her qualities, because without their intelligent upbringing she would not be what she is today.

This book is about Rachna's journey in Dessign7. Since I have seen her grow professionally only, I have restricted the content to her professional growth. I would assume that someone who has grown professionally so much over the last few years has definitely achieved greater milestones on the personal front, but Rachna will have to find someone more apt to write about those.

I am not a professional writer. I started by writing memos to congratulate Rachna on her growth in Dessign7. These memos expressed some of the most unforgettable incidents which helped Dessign7 soar to greater heights. But, eventually an incident which shook me up, ensured that it became a full-fledged book with a logical climax. So, if scholars of English feel that grammar or literature rules have been broken, please blame the software which did not highlight these mistakes in time.

So, let me begin from the end, the day I decided to write the book.

Contents

The End

1

I looked at the two ladies leave my cabin, as they slowly allowed the frosted glass door to close behind them. I looked around the cabin, a little lost in memories of yesterday's incident. I could still see vivid flashbacks of yesterday's event. I could see my cabin full of people, shouting abuses at each other while shedding tears. Images of people at loggerheads with each other. Friends and well-wishers I loved and cared for were flashing before my eyes, arguing like there was no tomorrow. I recognized the faces, although they appeared blurred through the tears in my moist eyes. I was hurt and shattered, strongly feeling the pain I had felt yesterday. All my questions were answered except for one, "What wrong had I done to suffer this torment?" I repeatedly asked myself the same thing. But I could neither find an answer to my question nor could I find the people who had the answer to my question. I could only find myself sitting in my empty cabin.

I snapped back to the reality of the empty room which I solely occupied. I glanced to the wall on my left which displayed my certificates and photographs, neatly composed against the white painted wall. I caught sight of one frame in particular and although I had written the poem myself, I felt like reading it again today. The title read "My First Earning" and below it was stuck a ten rupee note. The frame was a gift that I had given to Anagha, my wife, a few years ago, on her birthday. The ten rupee note was the topmost bill in the bundle of money she received as her first salary. And to immortalize it, I framed it, with a little inspirational poem written below it. Till this day, I have treasured it. My focus shifted for a couple of seconds as I heard a giggle outside the cabin and I saw the hazy silhouette of one of the ladies leave the office. Although the giggle distracted me, I was content knowing that someone in the office was happy. I continued to read my poem framed on the wall:

"With every growth, and every milestone,
With every obstacle that you cross,
Remember the spark that ignited the fire,
Always remember the very first.
Look forward to achieve greater tasks
March ahead to amass more and more,
But once a while, reflect on the past,
To take a look at your very first."

The words "Remember the spark that ignited the fire" haunted me, especially in context with yesterday's event. I journeyed deep into the past to remember the spark that ignited the fire. But ventured a little too deep into the past.

****

Since the age of three, I spent my childhood in Kuwait. I was a good student, almost a prodigy to my parents, and my father never spared any costs in ensuring that I received the best education. He went beyond his means when he registered me with New English School – the top -of -the-line Cambridge board school in Kuwait.

It is true that the early educative years are the formative years in one's life; and learning with the best also gave me a cultured perspective of life. I was trained to become a gentleman with a strong foundation in language, mathematics and sciences. Innovative ways of teaching serious subjects made learning a complete experience. In an era where rap music was at its peak, our class of thirty five students was divided into groups of five and each group composed and performed a rap song on one of the 'The Seven Systems of the Human Body'. We had chosen the digestive system. We wanted to add humor to our performance, so we made funny posters to complement our song. We won the first prize - a bag of fruits☺. Interactive teaching methods made learning fun and subconsciously I also began to like teaching. Learning and teaching became such an integral part of my character, that later in life, when I entered the business arena it gave me a competitive edge to expand my organization rapidly.

I was enjoying my life in Kuwait with my family until a minor turn of event called "The Gulf War" changed our fate. We shifted to Pune, Maharashtra, India. Since our shifting to India wasn't planned, we weren't carrying any 'certificates of our education' with us. Of course, we had our passports, but that didn't help me prove my educational qualifications to institutes. An unplanned migration to a new place made me realize the importance of having official documents. I understood that it's not so important to be educated as it is to be able to prove your qualification. Otherwise the authorities refuse to accept facts. Fortunately, the government eventually realized that there was a large number of such migrants and instructed schools and colleges to accept migrant students without a complete set of documents. So, I finally got admission into Wadia College, where I completed my high school. I also met Anagha there - my better half.

Life in India was an absolute contrast to life in Kuwait. In Kuwait, life was always air-conditioned. It was a weird adjective to describe my life, however, it was the most appropriate single word adjective I could think of. I woke up in air-conditioned bedrooms, went to school in our air-conditioned school buses, studied in our air-conditioned classrooms and then returned to our air-conditioned home. It was a well-cushioned life. I spoke to friends on the phone endlessly, discussing fancy cars and the latest computer games without having to worry about the phone bill. Once a while we celebrated birthday parties, but that was the only time I met friends outside school. As kids, we were not independently mobile and parents never had the time to socialize.

In India, people were more humble and down to earth. They were more social and spared leisure time for each other. They sought satisfaction within the smaller things in life. They loved to bargain a rupee for a bunch of bananas, even though their time spent bargaining was worth much more than that. They enjoyed street food for dinner after a casual evening walk with family. The more adventurous lot simply waited for a bus to leave the bus stand and then ran behind it to grab a foothold in it. Just like its color full flag, there were many colors of life yet to be explored by me in India.

Coming from a safe, conservative and secure environment, I found this lifestyle challenging. An average Indian's life is lived on the streets and to succeed here, you had to be street-smart. From my friends in Wadia College, I acquired street-smartness, but at the same time, I retained the polished attitude learnt from my British teachers. Later, this 'schizophrenic personality', as I always called it, helped me shape my career. In the field of interior designing, one not only has to deal with the client- who is rich, elite and cultured, but also has to manage the laborers- who at times can be quite crude. Whilst I was shaping my personality, subconsciously, I was laying the foundation for future success.

After completing school, I had short listed two career options - Hotel Management and Architecture. My career counsellor advised me to pursue hotel management. I even secured admission in the best hotel management college in the country, but it was my perception that a career in hotel management would be job-dependent, and that was a major drawback to me. Being brought up in a business family, I wanted to eventually start my own business, which seemed more feasible in the field of architecture. So, I went on to acquire a degree in Architecture.

I had grown ambitious with time and strived to become financially independent as soon as possible. After I completed the third year of the five-year architecture course, I started working part-time after college hours.

I even started executing small independent interior projects at meagre fees. Although these projects were not highly profit-generating, they gave me a lot of practical insight into the field. It also inspired creative ideas in my academic work. Owing to my hands-on experience, my college design portfolios improved in terms of my presentation of ideas and the technical viability of my design solutions. My fellow students made preliminary presentations of their conceptual sketches for me to assess the technical feasibility of their designs, before presenting them to the faculty. I enjoyed the teaching process.

As soon as I graduated from college, I worked as an intern with Ar. Amala Sheth, a prominent personality in the prestigious interior designers' circle of Pune. I trained with her for two long, hectic and exhaustive years, during which I learnt about detailing a concept to create a good design; using new materials innovatively; the intricacies of project management; accurately estimating a project cost and optimally managing a vendor's resource. I'll always credit her for my business acumen. Whilst working there, I also understood the standard of professionalism that a client demands and how to succeed in business by surpassing his expectation. But of course, it is well known that a cent percent satisfied client is a myth. What is lesser known is that a cent percent satisfied employee is also a myth.

I closely observed my colleagues to figure out how they perceived the company and what they expected from it. They were lured by the small perks they received, like additional travel allowance or an unexpected incentive on a project. It wasn't the salary, but this little extra money which motivated them to stick onto their job. Usually, it is the lack of growth in salary, authority or learning that is the major reason for employees to resign. I resigned for the same reason. Although I respected Ar. AmalaSheth, I resigned primarily because my request for a pay raise was rejected. I had a better paying, part-time job offer, leaving me with a few spare hours a day to undertake projects independently. It gave me the security of steady salary and opportunities to generate a little additional income.

It was during my tenure at Ar. Sheth, that I eventually exchanged my wedding vows with Anagha. I am a Muslim and she is a Hindu. Since we had both decided against converting from our respective religions, we decided to get married as per the Indian Marriage Act. We pledged our vows before the appointed registrar and we were married within a few minutes. On the same evening, we hosted a lavish reception to complete the ceremony. Close friends and family attended the function, wishing us luck to start a new chapter in our lives. Indeed, it was a landmark day in my life, which I'll always stop by and cherish whenever I travel down the memory lane.

After I resigned from Ar. Sheth's office, I took up employment as a project manager with M/s. Cube Contractors, a premier interior turnkey contracting company in Pune. There I learnt the intricacies of contracting. I started looking at a site from the viewpoint of a contractor, as compared to earlier when I would see the site from the eye of a designer. I developed skills to negotiate with a vendor or a sub-contractor either to reduce their price or get additional perks for free. Every rupee saved was a rupee earned. I maintained detailed inventory of all raw material that arrived on site and optimized material wastage to ensure maximum profit to the company. I closely monitored all the laborers and their methods of working to understand legitimate shortcuts we could use to expedite work on site. After all, time saved is money saved and money saved is money earned.

At every site, there was an ever-conflicting battle between the designer and us, the contractors. The designer's perspective of a site was very different from our expectation from the same site. He strived for perfection in design, cost being his last concern, whilst our primary motive was to optimize the cost of the project in order to ensure maximum profits for us. An ideal balance of these conflicts often benefitted the client. He ended up with a classy-looking place well within his budget. It was this ideal, value-for-money solution that fascinated me. I decided that someday, when I start my own company, I would neither be only a designer nor only a contractor. The model of my company would principally promote design-and-build solutions. Towards the end of the year I felt that I had gone beyond the learning curve offered by my current company and my ambition got the better of me. I ventured into my own business - Dessign7.

DESSIGN 7. The name of the company had its own short story. Since I was born on the 7th of July (the 7th month of the year), a prominent numerologist suggested that the number seven should be incorporated in the company name. So I adhered to it and christened our company DESIGN 7. To this, our lawyer objected citing that it could prove difficult to get this name registered for trademark, because it was a word in the English dictionary.

We added an additional 'S' to 'DESIGN'. The two 'S's next to each other also abbreviated to 'Shabbir Sabuwala' and the lawyer was finally comfortable registering our trademark on this name. Dessign7 was thus born and christened. And it did indeed proved lucky.

Shortly after launching our venture, our lucky charm, our daughter Shirin, was born. Anagha realized that Shirin would require more of her time and wanted to spend a substantial amount of her time monitoring her development. On the other hand, my business was at a nascent stage and any additional help was welcome. So, she left her job as an electronics engineer to partner with me in business. It allowed her to help me and yet keep her time flexible enough for Shirin.

The growing business eventually saw progress and with time we recruited a number of employees, some lasting longer than the others. But employee attrition was a constant problem and our search for new recruits was always ongoing. It was during one such search for fresh interior designers that I first met Rachna Vora.

Beginning of a Journey 2

It was sometime in the first week of May, a very regular day with only work and stress to look forward to. We had a continuous lack of staff and finding the right recruits was a task which made me look up to the HR guys as demigods. Also, I wanted my existing designers, Devika and Aaisha to have a promotion by giving them suitable juniors. The only ray of light in an otherwise bleak day was a call I received the day before from an accented, fast-spoken female voice, “Hello, I am an interior designer fresher, recently passed out of FIID and I was wondering if there was a vacancy in your firm.” Without betraying any anxiety, I requested the voice to come for an interview at 10:00 in the morning.

Weaving through the usual traffic, I made my way to the office, hoping to see the unknown face of a possible new recruit. As I entered my office, pre-occupied with mentally planning the schedule of the day, Zeenat - our front desk manager startled me with her pleasant “Good morning, sir”. I casually greeted her the same, as I quickly stole a glance to my right to see two fresh faces sitting on the two-seater sofa next to the pantry door. I swiftly made my way, past the reception and into my glass cabin where I settled myself into my chair, dialed a 308 on the phone and instructed Zeenat to send in the girls who had come for an interview.

The door opened and the girls walked in, each of them individually holding a file and a design portfolio. The tall, fair and slightly healthier girl introduced herself first.

"Hello sir, I am Palak Lalwani. I have recently completed interior designing from FIID. This is a portfolio of few of the works I have done," Palak introduced herself as she put her portfolio of A3-size drawings on the table for me to study. Having conducted numerous interviews by now, I had realized that the formality of going through a design portfolio was necessary to boost the morale of the candidate; however, it never really helped to select the right candidate. Anyone adequately experienced could easily spot a hundred technical mistakes in a school portfolio.

I questioned her about a basic drafting error, "So, Palak, do you think the drawing dimensions are legible?" She gave a confused look, nodded in agreement and muttered something, which I chose to ignore. I closed the portfolio and asked a few basic questions and assumed the interview closed. That's when I got a second portfolio on my table.

"Morning Sir, I am Rachna Vora and I have also recently completed Interior Designing from FIID and this is my portfolio." I looked at the direction of the voice to see Rachna Vora. Rachna was a short, maybe 5'3", tanned girl with flicks covering part of her forehead and a small cut mark near the chin. Dressed in a dark beige Indian top and jeans, she was an absolute contrast to her friend beside her. I would have otherwise finalized Palak's appointment, but since I was presented with the option of choosing a junior staff member, I quickly browsed through the second portfolio. Rachna learnt from her counterpart's experience and promptly said "Sir, even my portfolio has dimensions which might not be legible, but we were never corrected in college." I could identify with this statement. As a student, even I had encountered many professors who were so involved in ensuring that the requirements of the syllabus were met that they never concerned themselves with the practical aspects of learning. Rachna continued with her pro-active explanation, "But, I am sure under your esteemed guidance, we'll learn a lot and avoid such mistakes in the future." I was flattered by her remark and avoided pointing out further errors.

After going through both the portfolios and interacting with them, Rachna came across as a person with clarity in thought. She explained her concept in great depth, including the various finishing material that she had visualized to complete her designs. Also, she described the kind of paintings and artifacts that she would use to decorate the rooms. Although, few of her ideas were impractical due to either technical constraints, material availability or budget restrictions, I had rarely seen such clarity of thought with any fresher. Overall I felt she was very passionate about the field and sensed a learning spark within her. Also, I was impressed with the confidence with which she handled the interview. I clarified to them, "Since, we have only one vacancy at the moment, I would like to offer the position to Rachna. The stipend that we offer to a fresher is two thousand rupees per month and subject to your performance, it will be increased." I could immediately see the disappointment on their faces and added further, "If you want to learn, our office is the right place. You might feel the stipend is less but you will learn a lot and eventually, if you prove yourself, we will give you a raise. But at the moment I can't offer you more. Think about it and respond to me by tomorrow. We require someone to start immediately." We then thanked each other and they left, promising to revert by the same evening.

When Rachna did call that evening, it was to negotiate an increased salary. She explained to Anagha, my wife and partner in business, that she had better salary offers from other firms but wanted to join us because Dessign7 would offer a better learning experience. We, on the contrary, were short staffed and desperately needed to build our team. After discussing it with me, Anagha made her a counter offer of Rupees two thousand and five hundred per month. Rachna confirmed her appointment in Dessign7.

***

"The name is Vora, Rachna Vora." It was an introduction out of a James Bond movie. Although she never introduced herself like that to anyone - at least to none of our clients, her style quotient and her accent never indicated her incapability to introduce herself like that. So, I thought of it as an ideal introduction.

Rachna Vora, daughter of Chandrika and Nalin Vora, was born and brought up in Pune, Maharashtra, India.

Even though Pune is just a three and half hour drive from Mumbai, it boasts of a very pleasant climate. This was the primary reason for bigwigs from Mumbai to plan their weekend houses and retirement homes in Pune. Owing to this, Pune became popularly known as the 'Pensioner's Paradise'. In the late nineties, when Pune became an IT Hub, it saw a lot of progress and money inflow. But much before the IT revolution, Pune saw a greater revolution. On 27th April, 1985, Rachna Nalin Vora was born. Rachna is a sandwich – born between the elder sister, Disha, an IT professional and an artist, and the younger sibling, Pooja, a choreographer. Her father was a prominent contractor and had established a name for himself in the construction and real estate business, whilst her mother was a home maker.

Rachna did her schooling from Dastur School, one of the good-rated schools of early Pune; and I am quoting an extract from her own trumpet that she blew, "Our group was one of the most loved by all teachers in school." She was, from what I assume, a naughty kid who participated in a lot of activities, always maintained a good rapport with the teachers, and performed well academically. Being in the same school as her elder sister helped her create a positive first impression on all her teachers.

Once she was out of mid-school, she continued her education at Wadia College, a customary high-schooling destination for every fun-loving student in Pune. She graduated with a diploma in Mass Communication from RIM University, and later enrolled in FIID, Koregaon Park, for a two-student batch of Interior Designing. It was here that she met Palak Lalwani, her classmate first and then a close friend. Rachna was a people's person. She maintained a calm, composed and confident attitude because of which people wanted to befriend her in the initial interaction. Her care and compassion ensured that she was quick to make friends, and she truly valued every friendship, even if it meant going out of her way to accommodate them. This obviously did not mean that she was perfect. She had her share of mishaps.

One such mishap had almost cost Rachna her Diploma in Interior Design. It was towards the end of their course in interior designing that both Palak and Rachna were frustrated with the incompetency of their professor. In one of their angry SMS conversation, Rachna addressed their professor as "bitch" and instead of sending the SMS to Palak, she sent it to the professor by mistake. I had a hearty laugh when I first heard that.☺ After much counselling, the matter got solved and she passed out of FIID.

After passing out from the FIID, Rachna and Palak immediately landed a position as an interior designer with a leading modular kitchen manufacturing firm at an initial salary of rupees five thousand a month. Excitedly, they went for a movie at a newly opened multiplex to celebrate their appointment. It was an advertisement of Dessign7 which caught their attention. The photographs of various sites completed by Dessign7 impressed them and they realized that they would learn more with a main stream interior designing firm than a kitchen manufacturer. Since both of them had a fetish for learning, they called me up and fixed up an appointment for interview.

It was on 7th May 2007 that Rachna started her journey in Dessign7 and planted the seed for "The Growing Years."

****

Dessign7 was an interior design studio with a unique way of spelling 'Design'. Clients often corrected us on the spelling and my explanation to them normally worked as an effective ice-breaker. Of course, I never mentioned to them that the '7' in the name was simply associated with my birth date. I explained to clients and friends that 7 represents the seven colors of rainbow, seven notes of music and even the seven systems of the human body which are the sustainers of life. Clients who didn't know me were usually impressed with my philosophy, but close friends chose to ignore my explanation.

Dessign7 was my proprietary firm. The growth of Dessign7 was fast and steady, mainly attributed to the 24 x 7 efforts of Anagha, Rajesh and I. We started with a single desktop computer in the corner of my living room. We initially undertook small, petty interior works. Within a year of its establishment it grew from a home office to a 105-square-feet office in the basement of Pune's prime mall. Our efficiency and competitive pricing was our unique selling point. I had trained with one of the best designers in town, and therefore, I was aware of the latest design trends. I was a trained contractor so I knew how to optimize costs, and therefore, we quoted competitive prices to our clients. We received good references from the clients we serviced. Dessign7 executed a lot of projects in a short span of time. Eventually, we needed a larger premise for office expansion and to handle our rapidly growing business. We moved to an 1100 square feet office with a reception area, a waiting lobby, a large director cabin with an attached bedroom and toilet, a comfortable studio for eight designers with an attached toilet, a cubicle for Rajesh – now a team leader - and an oversized pantry cum diner.

We had worked hard day and night for the last seven years to bring Dessign7 to its current position, where we had sufficient ongoing assignments and scope for expansion was plenty. The major marketing and design activities were done by me, whilst Anagha looked after the administrative and advisory function. Rajesh was the pillar of support. He was the task man who would execute site work, coordinate with various vendors and contractors to ensure smooth flow of work on site and ensured that we met the committed deadlines. Client interactions, vendor selections and bill checking were my added responsibilities. We also had assistance from our two senior interior designers – Aaisha and Devika.

Aaisha, the senior-most designer at that time, was with us before we moved to our newest office. She was a short, fair and slightly egoistic person, who put in hard work double the measure of her physical stature. Her greatest professional thrill was to receive an appreciation letter from me for the hard work she put in. She was my second-most loyal and hardworking employee, only after Rajesh. She was passionate about her work and followed my instructions meticulously. Rajesh was much more senior than Aaisha and she completely accepted this seniority. She never challenged his decision; hence her bond with Rajesh was strong and their work chemistry was fairly synched. She took great pride in her successful execution of the tetrahedral false ceiling in the office reception. A design conceptualized by me, inspired from a crumpled sheet of paper, it was indeed a very complicated ceiling design to execute.

Devika was an absolute contrast to Aaisha, physically and emotionally. She was a plump girl with a sweet, round and smiling face, which never betrayed the turmoil within. An absolute rebel at heart, ready to defy every obstacle that came her way, she wanted to consciously challenge life. The only challenge that she avoided in life was solving a mathematics problem. She hated mathematics beyond expressions and avoided even simple addition and subtraction problems. I don't know how and why she landed in the field of interior designing, a field not only of creative concepts but also of measurement and calculations. Her emotional anchor was her once-upon-a-time colleague and now her boyfriend Shahnawaz. She would confront verbal challenge with a verbal assault and she would slash mathematical challenge with her sword of ignorance. Anything that didn't fit within her frame of mind was ignored and that is why she always ignored Rajesh.

***

Rachna was assigned as a common junior to Devika and Aaisha, for them to off load their basic drafting work. It was their job to train her in conceptualization, designing and drafting skills. The monotonous and laborious jobs were to be off loaded to her whilst they could concentrate more on creating better designs for the clients. The ripples of creativity are best formed in a calm mind.

Rachna's introduction to Devika was anything but pleasant. Zeenat opened the office at 10:00am every day and ensured that the maid gave us a clean work environment by 10:30am. Being the first day, Rachna walked into the office at 10:30 sharp and asked Zeenat for guidance. "Hi, I am Rachna, I am supposed to join office from today as a junior interior designer," Rachna said humbly. "Wait in the studio until one of the designers comes in," instructed Zeenat pointing to a vacant seat in the studio. Rachna seated herself on a vacant workstation in the studio, awaiting instruction from the seniors who were yet to walk in. Devika walked in five minutes later and immediately asked Zeenat for a "Travel Expense Statement" – a document used to record the monthly travel expenses incurred by staff and used to calculate their reimbursement. Zeenat, offended by her stern request, retaliated with, "I had already given it to you last month." Devika shouted back demandingly "Zeenat I want another one for this month. Just give me the damn sheet." A few loud remarks saw Zeenat giving a fresh copy of the expense sheet to Devika. No one ever won an argument with otherwise a very soft spoken Devika. For Rachna, Devika was established as a person not to be messed with.

Rachna received her initial assignment from Devika, of drafting elevations for Mr. Bapat's residence. She also explained the basic filing system, sources of other data which Rachna would require and of course, upon Zeenat's insistence, she explained the "Travel Expense Statement". Whilst Rachna was studying the drawings, Aaisha entered the studio and a squint of remembrance prompted her to question, "Are you from Dastur School? I remember you. Even I am from Dastur." Acting fast on the lead,

Rachna faked a recollection; they exchanged names of some common acquaintances, teachers and some other nostalgic moments. Rachna's journey kick-started in Dessign7.

Rachna did well from the beginning. She had good visualization skills, which are very important for a design professional. And to complement them, she had the creative flair required to be a good designer. A few days of review made me believe in her capability of accepting the challenge of handling a project independently. She also had an added advantage over her seniors, her communication skills were far better. Rachna exhibited the desire to learn and excel, which encouraged me to entrust her with scores of responsibilities, so when we bagged the corporate fit-out job for M/s Info-In-Network India Ltd, I asked her:

"We have to start working on Info-In-Network India Ltd. It's a fifteen thousand square feet corporate office. Do you want to handle the project on your own?"

"Yes sir, definitely", was the prompt and excited reply.

"You'll get to learn a lot, but it'll be a fast-track project with lots of hard work. Will you be able to handle that kind of pressure?" I warned her.

"That shouldn't be a problem." She assured me.

"The project will also demand waiting back late at night on site, will your parents be OK with that?"

"Don't worry," she said, "I am sure they will understand that this will be an important learning experience for me."

"Well then come with me to survey the site. Take the laptop. If you have any doubts there feel free to ask me on the way."

Throughout the next forty minutes, whilst we maneuvered our way through the disorganized Pune traffic enroute to the site, Rachna fired lots of questions and scribbled my answers in her diary. The only time that she remained quiet was whilst passing through a specific patch of road within a tunnel. I inquired the reason for the sudden silence and she confessed, "I suffer from claustrophobia, I hate tunnels, elevators and other tightly enclosed spaces."

"How come I have never seen you climb the office staircase, instead of using the elevator?"

Rachna gave a slight smile with a glee in her eyes.

"Watch out Rachna!" I shouted to break the silence, "The tunnel will collapse!"

Rachna went pale. She broke into cold sweat. I panicked.

"I was kidding, just kidding. Chill." I laughed and reassured her.

Rachna was breathing heavily. I quickly drove out of the tunnel and she regained her breath. Slowly, she got back to her questioning mode and restarted inquiring about the site.

By the time we reached site, she was educated of the client's name, the nature of their work, their staff requirements, our past history with the clients, and the number of various types of contractors that would be required for her to line up to execute the job. On site, I had already asked our electrical contractor, Rahul, to be present to assist us with the site measurements. I entrusted Rachna with the task of taking the site measurements with Rahul, whilst I finished my meeting with the company directors. It was slightly risky to depend upon a first timer for the task, but ability is best judged by the responsibility handled. Just like no man is a criminal until proven guilty, for me no one is incompetent until proven so. I trusted people easily.

An hour later, Rachna joined me with the measurements drafted on the laptop, ready for me to verify them on site. Except for minor errors, which could be easily forgiven for a first timer, she did very well. I had seen the spark in her and she had lived up to my expectations with her very first independent assignment. I was already glad that I had shown faith and assigned the project to Rachna.

I came back to the office and shared my thoughts with Aaisha and Devika, "This new girl Rachna seems to be smart. She managed to take the entire site measurement on her own, only with Rahul's help. I am thinking of letting her handle the project on her own. What do you guys think? What's your feedback about her?"

Devika spoke, least bothered by my decision, "Yeah let her handle it, no problem. We'll anyways monitor it to prevent any drastic errors."

Aaisha,although, seemed a little skeptical, "Do you think she'll be able to handle the entire project on her own? It's a prestigious project and she's just a fresher, if you want I'll handle it."

"No! You are already overloaded with work," I spoke to Aaisha, listing down the projects she had on hand. "I think she'll manage it and like Devika said, I'll monitor it. Let's see how well she handles pressure."

"Ok, if you think so. But I can handle it if you want." Aaisha's seniority seemed hurt and threatened. She knew she would have been my first choice to manage this project if Rachna was not there. After all, she enjoyed the privilege of getting 'an appreciation letter' from me. But my preference had changed and Aaisha sensed it. She became a little insecure.

***

Anagha and I were happy with our latest recruit and foreseeing the inflow of work, we immediately decided to hire another fresher. I remembered Rachna's friend Palak, who had accompanied her at the time of her interview.

"Your friend who had accompanied you for interview, is she working somewhere?" I asked Rachna

"Well, she's working with Sanjay Thorat," Rachna answered. Sanjay Thorat was a respectable name in the local architectural community. He bagged most of the crème-de-la-crème projects in the city. He ran a big organization with huge workforce and followed traditional hierarchical systems. Only the senior project managers, with proven loyalty towards the firm, were allowed to interact with the clients and contractors. The young designers were allotted basic drafting work or filing of papers along with other administrative work. Because of this, the learning for a fresher in his office was very slow. I always felt that such large design organizations, seldom gave the desired exposure and responsibility to the new employees.

"Why do you ask about Palak?" Rachna asked.

"Yeah, we were thinking of replacing you," I quipped.

"Sir is not happy with your performance on the Info-In-Network India Ltd's office project," Aaisha added with a sarcastic smirk.

Rachna was about to retort but I intervened, "Just kidding Rachna. You are doing pretty fine," I reassured her. "Actually, our work load is increasing and we were thinking of hiring one more person."

"Palak might be willing to join us. She has been complaining that she's not getting enough design exposure there. Most of the time she's handling calls at the reception. Let me ask her if she wants to come aboard," Rachna smiled, happy at the thought of reuniting with her friend.

"Well, if she's interested ask her to come tomorrow morning," I requested, then continued to announce, "As a matter of fact we might have to stay back late today and finish off Info-In-Network India Ltd's presentation."

That evening, we stayed back late in office and completed the presentation. Once the presentation was complete, we realized that we had pending obligation to our hungry stomachs and it was already quite late for us to return home, expecting our respective families to prepare dinner for us. Anagha, Shirin and I were anyways planning to order in food, owing to the hectic day's schedule, so we decided to order pizzas for everyone. Anagha's planning and Pizza Hot's thirty minutes delivery promise, ensured that we had pizzas for dinner after completing the presentation work. Before we parted for the day, I recapped the entire presentation with Rachna ensuring that nothing was left to the last minute for the following day.

"Did you speak to Palak for joining us?" was my parting question to Rachna.

"I spoke to Palak; she's coming to office at 9:00 tomorrow. I know it is a little early but she has to reach her office by 10:00. You'll be there, right?" Rachna replied and returned another question in exchange.

"Yes, I'll come early. Anything to finally find a replacement for you," I laughed as, we locked the office for the day.

It's amazing what a pizza can do for the office. It acts as a very tasty junk food, which can be ordered in as an afterthought at the end of a busy day. It also serves as a cause for sitting around, catching up on office and work gossip, to increase the bonding amongst people. But I never perceived it as a catalyst for HR activity. Till date that is. Palak came for an early morning interview and told me that she was not happy with her work profile at Sanjay Thorat. She was restricted to administrative and receptionist's work owing to her command over English. She was looking for something more educative and based on the feedback she had received from Rachna, she felt that Dessign7 was the right platform to learn. She accepted the job offer with a promise to join the following day. Our core design team for the next few years was complete. The core team with whom we spent 'The Glorious Years'.

Months later I learned that the empty pizza boxes lying outside the office impressed Palak as she thought "guys in this office are really chilled out and they party."

3 The Pillar of Support

Rajesh Chaudhary was a pillar of support.

Rajesh was unaware of the new development in the office over the last few weeks. After the successful completion of Primus Communications' office fit-out at Coimbatore, Rajesh had come back to the office only after a month. Surprised and shocked to see the new faces occupy the two vacant positions in a row of four workstations, he raised a questioning eyebrow to Aaisha, who was his only hope for an answer. Devika would have obviously ignored him. He looked at Aaisha across his cubicle, the largest workstation in the studio, and inquired about her work schedule as he occupied his chair. He got introduced to the two young ladies, explained his seniority in the firm and closed with the statement, "Any difficulties have you, come to me. OK?" Palak and Rachna nodded in agreement. Rajesh quickly turned to Rachna and instructed in a commanding voice, "You know to burn CD properly? Burn CD of Aman's Folder quickly." Although a little offended by his tone of speaking, Rachna nodded and commenced upon the task given.

Logical reasoning, ability to work hard, communication skills and moral values are some of the ingredients of any human soul that determine its strengths and weaknesses. Their proportions determine the flavor of every person. Everyone is good at one thing or the other, but to determine one's strengths and apply them in the right place is what eventually leads to success.

Just like mathematics baffled Devika and ego was Aaisha's weakness, communication skills and etiquettes were Rajesh's mysteries. His background and upbringing never brought him even close to these finesses of life. Although he appreciated the English language, he never really managed to grasp the intricacies of grammar. Listening to his constructed sentences was like canoeing down a rocky river. You eventually understood him, but the ride was rough. However, this never deterred him from making a bold and confident attempt. The two ingredients that summed up his personality were boldness and confidence.

I had met Rajesh, before starting my business, during my last job. He was a handyman, who was employed to do various miscellaneous tasks. He would deliver courier, fix any loose wiring, tighten screws of any loose hinges and in his spare time pester me to teach him some basics about interior designing. When the company bagged a major interior project for Army Institute of Technology, I was assigned as a project manager for that project. Since I was already impressed with Rajesh's dedication towards learning, I requested the directors if I could deploy him on site. With a little hesitation, they agreed and promoted him as a trainee site supervisor. Thus, Rajesh started his career in this field.

I had personally trained Rajesh to understand designs and read drawings, explain the same to contractors, material inventory management, and to ensure that contractors follow prescribed timelines. Being bold, he managed the sites well and being confident, he never shunned responsibility.

When I left my job, Rajesh resigned as well and joined me. Over the next few months, I trained Rajesh in design and drafting skills. I taught him the etiquette to handle contractors and showed him ways to improve rationing of material on site. He was a dedicated learner and was committed to his job. He would wait by my side on site, late night as well, to ensure all work was completed on time. He mastered the designing software and could draft a site plan, add dimension to a drawing, get a printout of it and give site clearances to contractors independently. Apart from conceptualizing a design or communicating with the clients or striking sales with prospective clients, Rajesh could handle almost anything. There were times when he could get adamant, but I knew how to handle him and could push him in the right direction with ease. Over the next couple of years, he proved his efficiency and grew to be my most trusted employee.

Anagha and I took an active interest in improving his personal life also. We enrolled him in a public speaking and personality development class, hoping to improve his client communication, but in vain. We took him shopping for formal clothes to replace the torn jeans and T-shirts he sported. We loaned him substantial money to get himself a bike, since he was ineligible for a bank loan, but eventually we waived it off. We even assisted him in marrying a Catholic girl he had fallen in love with. Our support was reciprocated with great loyalty from his side. The Indian culture promotes a lot of respect for the teacher, and Rajesh's affection towards me was legendary proof of this.

Respect, affection and loyalty are the right ingredients for being a pillar of support, but an essence of flowery language and finesse are essential for being in the forefront of any organization today. And that quality Rajesh's crude behavior could never adapt to. He marched ahead with his bold and confident behavior, neglecting the importance of communication and etiquette.

I on the other hand neglected that boldness and confidence cook the broth of ambition. And ambition can undermine the foundation of any pillar.

The Glorious Years 4

Growth of an organization is directly proportional to the growth of its people: growth in wealth, power and intellect. This growth has to be desired, attracted and seized by one.

*****

Growth of any organization is dependent on two major factors; firstly, the efficiency of its people, and secondly, the bond amongst its people. In short, in a people centric world, people are the most important. I always felt that "people buy people first and then their services". For a healthy growing organization, its staff has to be happy with the work environment. People have to be comfortable working cohesively with one another. Unfortunately, Rajesh was too brash, Aaisha was egoistic and Devika was an introvert. They were working together but were not bonding with one another at a personal level. I was depending on one of the two new recruits to form a connecting thread amongst the staff.

Rachna was warm and caring, which made it very easy for her to win friends. Within a week of her joining, she had befriended Devika – who was also a Taurean. Rachna and Aaisha were school mates. They had common acquaintances and gossiping about the nostalgic days strengthened their bond. Rachna and Palak were already good friends. Rajesh was a senior and Rachna respected that. She related with everyone in the office.

A couple of months after she joined, it was 7th of July, my birthday. On learning this, she exclaimed

"Wow! Exciting! So what do you guys normally do?"

"Nothing", replied Aaisha.

"Well, let's do something then. Quick! Before sir comes to office."

***

Anagha, Shirin and I had breakfast at The Taj - a five star property serving a wide spread of buffet breakfast. It was our own special way of celebrating birthdays within the family. Shirin gifted me a birthday card made personally by her. I was eager and excited to see the contents of the folded chart paper. The front cover had a cartoon of me holding her hand. I was identified by the striped red and white shirt and a stubble which I sported at times. "To My Loving Daddy" were the words on top, neatly sketched in blue crayons. Inside was a collage of adjectives which she used to describe me. As soon as started reading the words, she said, "Daddy, you know I went through the dictionary to find adjectives to describe you. There is one adjective starting from every alphabet."

"Wow Shirin! I am proud of you." I said whilst I was reading the carefully selected words.

"I didn't find any word with 'Q' and 'X', so those are missing."

"This is beautiful!" I hugged her, as I passed the card to Anagha to browse through it.

Next was Anagha's turn to give her gift. She brought out from within her purse a medium size box, very well gift-wrapped in golden foil. By the size of the box, I gauged it to be a watch. I was thrilled. I gathered patience and neatly opened the foil, appreciating the effort that Anagha had taken to wrap the gift. I opened the box to discover the piece. It was a 'RADO'!

"This is gorgeous! It's from their new collection of metallic black. Saw an ad in the newspaper the day before and thought of buying it myself." I screamed in excitement.

"I know. I saw you look at the ad. I thought you'd like it." Anagha said. She was well aware of my passion for collecting watches. I put on my new watch, gave a gleaming smile and showed it to her. It was perfect.

***

Post breakfast, we decided to stop by at the office for a couple of hours. The excited staff walked into the cabin with a huge, white box and the big blue envelope.

"Happy Birthday!" All of them shouted in a chorus.

I was just recovering from the surprise, when Rachna held up a golden crown and said, "This is the birthday crown for the birthday boss!" After an initial hesitation, I wore the crown as gesture to appreciate their enthusiasm.

Next Palak produce a circular, blue badge with frills and a white sticker which read "It's my BIRTHDAY!!!" and she said, "Go ahead sir, pin it up!" Anagha helped me pin up the badge to the shirt pocket.

Then Aaisha produced an oversized, gold-colored spectacles without any lenses, but instead they had huge dollar signs. I put on those as well.

Devika presented the big blue envelope. I opened it and removed a greeting card with "Happy Birthday to a Great Boss!" embossed on it. Inside the card, each one of them had written a personal message and signed it. Lastly, Rajesh and Zeenat produced a birthday cake with a lit candle on top. Everyone sang the birthday song in a chorus, whilst I blew the candle and cut the cake. As soon as the cake was cut, I fed a piece of cake to everyone, starting with Anagha. By the time I reached Rachna, she took a little icing on the finger and said, "Excuse me, but celebration demands it!" She giggled and smeared the chocolate cream on my face. The suit followed by everyone. I could here various random comments:

"Cream is good for the skin!"

"Yeah! It acts like a moisturizer!"

"Ma'am, Your turn! On the nose!"

"Mummy pick me up, even I want to put on his face!"

"Stop! His face is fully covered!"

"Thanks Rajesh!" I said.

"No, the forehead is left! Devika put a little cream on the forehead!"

"Get that cherry, for the nose!" Anagha said.

Aaisha put a cherry on the nose. Everyone stopped after ensuring that my face was completely smudged and posed for a group photo. Mobile phone cameras clicked as I modeled with varied combination of people and finally completed the ordeal of thoroughly cleaning my face.

Everyone was sitting with their pieces of cake by the time I returned from the washroom. Rachna said, "Did you have fun sir? Sorry if we went overboard."

"Definitely fun. Now you wait and watch out for your birthday!"

"Long time to go, 27th April by the way." Rachna grinned.

"Seriously, Thanks guys. The card is also lovely!"

"Sir, let's plan for a picnic!" Palak suggested.

"Palak, let's do a little work before we go vacationing!" I said.

"Maybe on one of the weekends," Anagha said.

"I no come on Sunday. One day get to rest," Rajesh interrupted.

"Fine. Then we can comfortably book an 8 seater. Otherwise with more people coming, we'd have to book an 11 seater." Rachna quipped, happy about the omission.

"OK. You go, but complete your work and go." Rajesh stared offensively at Rachna.

"It'll be on a Sunday, Rajesh. All sites and no fun will make Rajesh a dull boy!" Devika said.

"I have some work. I'll go and finish," Rajesh got up and left the rendezvous a little less excited than before.

"So besides, birthdays and picnics, what do you guys enjoy?" I asked.

"I love board games," Palak answered promptly.

"Yeah, we should get a few games like Pictionary, Life or Taboo in office," Rachna said.

"So when will we work?" Aaisha asked, defending Rajesh's line of thought.

"During the time that you spend on phone, we are working. She's constantly on phone with her hand covering her mouth. Aaisha likes to have secret conversations with someone." Devika retorted.

"Yes!" Rachna and Palak chorused. Rachna continued, "She is continuously having these secret conversations. Probably her boyfriend. She's always shouting on him."

"So what's your problem?" Aaisha yelled.

"Ok, break it guys. When do you want to plan the picnic?" I asked.

⁂

Rachna's initiative had two positive influences. Firstly, it set a trend of lavishly celebrating birthdays in office, which led to a strong bond amongst everyone. This tradition is followed to date even though the faces have changed.

Secondly, it led me to think that people performed better in teams rather than handling a project independently.

I started believing that if two people with complementary abilities were working on a project together, their individual perspective would help minimize the designing and execution flaws. Based on this theory, I formed teams with the four designers to handle any assigned project in a pair. I preferred one of the seniors to team up with one of the juniors for a healthy working. By default, since Rachna and Aaisha were school mates I preferred to team them up. They bonded like fire and water but I thought the combination would be interesting. I always did prefer to move people out of their comfort zones, and pairing Rachna and Aaisha was definitely going to shake them out of theirs. The individual teams would together handle the complete designing of the site assigned to them. They would research on latest technology and new finishing materials, incorporate them into innovative concepts, conceptualizea feasible design based on these concepts and prepare effective presentations for the clients after receiving my approval on the entire scheme. They would even present their designs to the clients, along with detailed explanation of their concepts. Rajesh, on the other hand, would supervise the site execution of both the teams, at the macro level, to ensure that they were optimizing the use of material on site, they had the requisite contractors to execute the work, and that they were issuing timely clearances on site.

Quick learners seldom wait for time to impart education. As time flew by, Rachna and Palak raced ahead to establish their proficiency in the firm. They researched well, to create chic and fresh concepts along with their senior counterparts. A special privilege that Rachna enjoyed was to get training imparted by me directly, during the fast-track project of Info-In-Network India Ltd, thereby improving her project management skills as well. Rajesh was the only other staff who had received such personal guidance from me in the past. Rachna and Palak scaled their way up to be on par with their seniors; with equal responsibility, graduated salaries and the power to discuss and overrule their designs. Eventually, Rajesh's contribution to designing was restricted only to ensure timely completion of work.

Seniority and superiority are synonymous to the word 'ego', without which the definition of ego is not complete. And the funny part is that what is most shaken by 'ego' also begins with an 'S' -one's 'stability' in an organization. When juniors grow fast, the seniors grow egoistic; a universal rule with few exceptions. Devika was devoid of such egoism and worked in perfect harmony with Palak; but Rachna's teammate Aaisha wasn't. Aaisha didn't realize it initially, but Rachna was a fast learner constantly willing to accept a challenge, understand it and logically resolve it - a trait which Aaisha was trying hard to keep pace with. She was constantly trying to prove herself better than Rachna and that was a lot of hard work for her. On a few occasions, she criticized Rachna's design concepts which were inspired by famous designer and accused her of plagiarism. I explained to her that every concept in any creative field is inspired by some source. We as designers ensure that we add our own unique touch to the inspiration and modify it substantially to create a new design. Aaisha understood me but couldn't accept it. She knew Rachna was becoming the new favorite in the office. Rachna was bettering herself every day and Aaisha wasn't able to keep pace with her. Aaisha felt my appreciation of her effort was reducing. She could see her unchallenged position in the organization losing stability. Rajesh, on the other hand, was far more experienced and confident to be shaken up by such growth. His position was always unchallenged and he never feared losing it. But his job profile had now evolved to supervising the growing teams; and supervision often leads to arguments; proving your point in an argument creates friction; and friction gives rise to ego.

"The Growth of an organization depends on the efficiency of its people and the bond amongst the staff." But juniors' efficiency can create and inversely affect the bond with the seniors. Therefore, I realized that as an organization evolves, a third parameter also contributes to the growing organization - establishing hierarchy. Devika and Aaisha were seniors but Rachna and Palak's efficiency forced me to dissolve the grading. Seniors were no longer seniors and juniors were no longer juniors.

***

The design teams established were working smoothly except for professional arguments from time to time. And we were running a flat organization with no hierarchy, with everyone sharing a good rapport with each other. We celebrated all birthdays and occasionally went out for dinners followed by late night movies. Ignorantly, Palak raised the bar of birthday treats with her very first grand treat, and no one ever dared to compete. She celebrated her birthday, the 9th of April, at Mia Chong China - a fine dining Chinese restaurant, with a bill so fine that she complained about it for months together. Other birthday treats soon followed. We explored various cuisines offered by various restaurants. This was the time in our lives where McDonalds had become the basic necessity of life, owing to Palak's fondness of it and occasionally when boredom of junk food overcame us, we decided to have pizzas – which was less junk than burgers, or so we believed. These were "The Gorging Years" in our life.

All of us shared a unique fetish for board games and once in a while took time out from our busy schedules to enjoy a spectrum of intellectual and non-intellectual games. Every game had its peak of favoritism, with different patented actions and dialogues associated with every game. The playing phase started with UNO. I am sure, everycard fan would have definitely come across UNO. It's a card game where each player's objective is to be the first one to discard all his cards. But of course, if he fails to say "UNO" while placing the second-last card, then he attracts the penalty of picking up an extra card. Although the game is to be played individually, conspiracy always foiled the player close to the end. Cheating was generally accepted sportingly, but once in a while one of us, usually the losing player, would throw a tantrum along with all cards on the table declaring others as cheaters. That would mark the end of the game for that day. Another day, another mood would see the beginning of another round of UNO, with the same cheaters.

We also indulged in dumb games, played in teams. Not that the games were dumb - in fact they were quite intellectual - but dumb because we had to be mute or refrain from directly using the word or expression we were trying to explain to our team members. Dumb charades, Pictionary and Taboo fell into this category. For Dumb charades, we hunted forlorn movie titles on Google and watched the members of the other team ape their way into winning or losing the game. Taboo was another team game where we sat in circle and every player was flanked by two members of the other team – one to keep a watch on time and the other to press the squeaky if a tabooed word was spoken. Pictionary put our drawing skills to test as we attempted to explain words through the medium of art. Papers were torn and pencil nibs broken to explain words to clueless team members. The anxiety and eagerness on everyone's face to comprehend their fellow member was priceless. The desperation and frustration of the player to make himself understood was also priceless. We played seriously, aggressively and flawlessly. We pounced on anyone trying to cheat, which included everyone eventually at one time or the other. But these team games enriched our spirits, our bond and our memories.

My personal favorite game, which didn't enrich our bonds, was Truth and Dare. We didn't spin a bottle, the conventional way of choosing victims. Instead we went in turns. We always gave the victim the option of choosing between answering a truth and doing a dare, but none of us ever dared to choose the latter. I guess we were never sure how low the others could stoop with a dare, so saying the truth was always a better option. We asked each other personal, awkward questions which we answered with perfect honesty, or so I like to believe. The idea of the questions was to embarrass the player and the best way to achieve this was to ask blunt questions concerning their colleagues. But honesty in games didn't matter; what mattered was the fun. Another game which grew to be a favorite was Life. More than playing the actual game of Life, we enjoyed the betting spree in the game. High stakes of unreal money were gambled to turn the tables around. These were times in Dessign7 when our daughter Shirin also enjoyed with the girls, whom she lovingly and respectfully addressed as "Didi". These were "The Gaming Years" in our life.

With all the fun and frolic,we worked very hard as well to deserve the fun. I conducted internal training sessions on various topics ranging from giving clearances on site to accurately incorporating the required dimensions to complete a working drawing. As the girls were independently handling sites, I explained to them the importance of maintaining window and skirting levels and customizing individual drawings as per these. We gradually improved the quality of drawings issued to contractors and thereby found that site execution was streamlining well, hence, requiring lesser supervision. These were "The Glowing Years" in our life.

I trained the teams on soft skills and conducted workshops on presenting designs and drawings to clients. I demonstrated the effectiveness of using ornate language to explain a design concept to the client, which they adopted with ease. Rachna and Palak always had better communication skills, and therefore, took the lead in the presentation made by the teams to their respective clients.

When people get too comfortable challenges are lost; so to keep the interest alive we did a lot of shuffling within the teams so that each could adapt to a different person's working style, and hence, learn more. Being pushed out of the comfort zone did create resistance, but we all believed in the saying "The Boss is always right"; or at least I did. Continuous counseling was given to improve communication with contractors, being specific with vendors whilst placing material orders, getting realistic timelines from contractors and ensuring they adhere to it, negotiating with vendors, bill checking, and developing customer relations.

The pleasures of teaching someone are immense. It not only teaches the student but also acts as a good revision for the teacher itself, not to mention that it also teaches you how to teach. Through the course of teaching the girls, I awoke to the fact that I loved teaching and would want to pursue it as a career someday. I realized that I am an educationalist and although the right training can create future competitors, it never really deterred me from trying to train the staff to be the very best. The outcome of my sincerity was thrilling – it started a new tradition in the office. The girls started a tradition to celebrate "Teacher's Day" on the 5th of September every year to appreciate my teaching skills. These were the "The Graduating Years" in our life.

This phase in the life of Dessign7, full of fun, food and learning might or might not return again but I'll always remember these years as "The Glorious Years".

The Educative Years 5

"The Glorious Years" of Dessign7 would be incomplete without highlighting some of the milestones in Rachna's career. These initial years of learning laid the foundation of her career as a designer, which later helped to her to metamorphose into an entrepreneur.

Her biggest and most challenging project at that time was Info-In-Network India Ltd.'s fifteen thousand square feet corporate office, with central air conditioning, false ceiling, lighting systems and computer networking seamlessly integrated with electrical wiring and furniture systems. Not to mention that all of this was to be completed within a choking timeline. Rachna had never handled such a mammoth project before,thus making it a superb learning experience for her. But what was even more exciting was the slow pace at which corporate companies gave approvals and yet expected you to perform without time escalations. Rachna learned the importance of allotting endless hours to clients, over snacks and coffee, and still conclude the meeting without any productive decisions. The officials discussed a lot, understanding the pros and cons of every alternative, but at the end of it the decisions were not given for the want of a senior's approval. Her puzzled expression always questioned "So what did we achieve during this meeting? Why couldn't we directly discuss it with the seniors? At least we would have got clearances." Of course at that point of time she wouldn't dare ask me that in so many words. But eventually she understood the bureaucracy of the corporate world. She realized that the knowledge which we imparted to the officials was explained to the seniors as their own research. This was a way to substantiate their positions in the company.

Another elusive trait of the corporate world is their speed over the internet. Before we reached office after every such unproductive meeting, we would receive a new list of site clearances required and how our delayed response could hamper the progress of work on site. And it always baffled us why these queries didn't dawn upon them just half an hour ago. My only explanation to Rachna would be, "Clients have a lot of time to spend on the internet, isn't it? If only they spend half of that time focused on work, they would get more productive results." We were the 'Actual site people' - as the industry labelled us - and sitting in office writing e-mails was not an affordable luxury. Rachna understood this. A client's job was to write queries on e-mail and our job was to solve his query, design accordingly, take approvals from him, convey the same to the contractors and ensure they finished work on time accommodating all changes and keeping the client "in the loop" all the time. And Rachna definitely agreed with this. It was her first lesson in the importance of communication in the interior designing industry.

Her second lesson in communication was imparted during the execution of the interior works for Spicecream–an ice-cream lounge designed by us. The site execution came at time when I had to travel for business development to Singapore, China and Hong Kong. Rachna was supposed to handle the site under the able guidance of Rajesh. Being better at communication, it was her responsibility to seek any decisions or approvals from the client directly. She was supposed to take an approval on the client's decision from Rajesh and execute it on site accordingly. It was a fast-track site on the execution front, with only fifteen days to finish the complete execution, without any guidance from me and ensuring that there is no budget inflation.

Rachna tried to adhere to the project schedule but got stuck for timely clearances on site. When Rajesh learnt about the delay, he was furious, "Rachna, why the hell the site is getting delayed?"

"The client cannot decide whether the furniture polish would look better in a glossy or a matt finish. So only the polish work is remaining," Rachna explained.

"But sir told you to speak to him. We are tight on schedule. You get his approval quickly and complete site." Rajesh exclaimed.

"I tried to convince him but he is not ready to take a decision. What can I do?" Rachna spoke timidly.

"If you can't do anything, then why you even work here. Go home and I'll ask someone else to handle the site." Rajesh shouted in frustration, "Sir will come back and ask me. He will not ask you!"

Rachna was hurt by Rajesh's anger and burst into tears. But Rajesh was cold to such emotions. He shrugged her off saying, "Don't cry for little things. Be tough not cry baby."

Finally Rachna and Rajesh together, could not convince the client for his decision and the project was stalled till the time I was back. I offered a very simple solution. I simply prepared samples of the available polish finishes and presented it to the client. Having the samples in front of him helped him to visualize the final effect. He immediately gave his decision. For all future projects Rachna realized that on-site sampling with short listed options given to the client is the best way to get timely approvals. It was her second lesson in the importance of communication.

Any interior design project has three main aspects, namely, creative designing, accurate execution and flawless communication. Creative designing is subjective and varies with every individual's preference. Accurate execution is often the onus of the contractor appointed for the job, although we have to monitor him closely. Flawless communication is most essential aspect for good project management. Mastering communication and closing the communication link is the most important. A piece of information received by us has to be conveyed to all the concerned parties and any feedback or decision on it also has to be communicated to all the people concerned.

A simple instruction which people fail to follow. It can create huge heaps of misunderstanding amounting to time and cost over-runs, which are usually borne by the party weakest in the communication link. Rachna learnt her lesson in sealing her communication links from the initial few projects.

The second important aspect of the business is creative designing. I had assigned the interior designing of Mr. Sandeep Mulchandani's bungalow, located in the prestigious vicinity of Koregaon Park, to Rachna and Devika. As a team, they were expected to conceptualize the entire design and present their ideas to me before we pitched the designs to the client. They spent the entire week allotted to them researching endlessly on the internet to come up with a few creative concepts. They showed the concepts to Rajesh for an initial feedback but he brushed it aside saying, "Sir not like these designs. You see sir's design. You need a little round or some curve. This is all is so simple and straight lines. Why you need designer to do this? Change it!"

Rachna and Devika were taken aback by his comments. They had spent an entire week working on concepts which would be rejected. They were wondering whether their designs were completely off-track. But due to lack of time, they couldn't change them. They mustered enough courage to show them to me. Rachna started her presentation by explaining the master bedroom design, "We are planning to have a suspended looking bed, with a broad ledge on the foot board side for seating. We'll use an innovative material for the bed-back, perhaps copper metal with strips of wooden inlay, keeping the lines straight and simple. It'll look elegant. The inlay can continue on to the false ceiling as well." Rachna waited for my comments.

"Continue with other room designs," I spoke, preoccupied with visualizing the design in my mind.

"For the living room, we were thinking of using black glass. It'll go well with the lounge-like ambience that Mr. Mulchandani desires," another pause followed. They looked for any reactions from me but were disappointed with my blank expressions. Then Rachna finally continued, "Their daughter has a keen interest in music and she's fond of various musical instruments. So, we thought we'll create a theme room for her. We'll have a music piece which starts on the wardrobe and continues on the ceiling. A room full of musical notes and instruments will be the ideal concept her bedroom." After a short interval, Rachna spoke, "We spend too much time working on these concepts, so we could not complete the other two rooms and the kitchen designs." She continued and asked hesitatingly, "How are these ideas?" I could see traces of nervousness in her pauses.

Finally, Devika asked, "Are these OK, good, bad? We know they are all simple and straight lines but we think that it'll look elegant. If you want we can work along some other lines also. What do you think?"

My silence was making them anxious. They were awaiting my reaction, but I was trying to visualize the designs and analyze the concept. After a lot of thought, I finally spoke, "These concepts are simply," I paused a little to create suspense, "Beautiful! Simply beautiful! The designs are simple, elegant and Sandeep will definitely like it. Finalize the drawings for these three rooms. He'll be coming tomorrow for a meeting. We can show these three rooms to him and ask him for a week's extension for the other areas." Devika and Rachna were thrilled with my reaction. On their way out I congratulated them by saying "Great job both of you!" They thanked me for my appreciation and started finalizing the designs for their presentation the next day.

Rachna had displayed ample talent and she had the confidence to follow her will. Although it was a joint effort, Devika being a senior, had never before come up with such innovative concepts. Rachna had started to master the complexities of a good design. She adopted the right inspiration for conceptualizing a design; developed the inspiration with appropriate material finishes and scaled the concept perfectly within the available space to create a holistic design experience.

And to reiterate what I felt, even Mr. Mulchandani approved the designs immediately, without even demanding an alternative.

There were even times when I didn't like the designs which Rachna created. Designing is a subjective field, where individual choices vary drastically. It didn't matter whether a certain design suited my palate, as long as the client happily approved it.

Even to this day, I do not like the design Rachna and Palak created for Nainika Verma's daughter's room. On the wardrobe, they had a white butterfly embossed on a metallic purple background with a trail of circles left behind. I felt it was too graphical and not apt for furniture design. I had already predicted that Nainika would not like it and suggested to them to change the concept. But Rachna wanted the challenge of convincing her, demanding one chance to present the design. I gave her that chance. I had already spent various sessions imparting training and conducting mock-ups on how to present design concepts to clients. The time to test the effect of my training had come. Rachna was using her best language that day. She used extravagant, floweryverses to describe her design. She was generous in her use of words like 'classy', 'beautiful' and 'lively', to give a verbal walkthrough of their design to Nainika. Finally, Rachna not only presented the design to Nainika but also got it approved by her. Rachna's presentation skills had improved.

The third important aspect of our business is accurate site execution. We appoint various labor contractors who are assigned different tasks on site depending upon their field of expertise. Their job is to provide laborers and manage them on site to ensure that they work efficiently within the prescribed timeline. They are also responsible for guaranteeing quality workmanship. As part of site management, Rachna's job was also to explain the design properly to the contractor on site. Her communication skills were ideal to interact with a client, but laborers often didn't comprehend her. Rajesh always complained, "What that Rachna speaks, no laborers understand. Then they ask me and I have to explain everything again."

I always felt that Rachna spoke too fast for the contractors to understand her. In addition to that, she had a minor British accent which made matters worse. I repeatedly told her on various sites, "Speak slowly and continuously observe the contractor's expression to see if he has understood you. Take long pauses in between the explanations for him to absorb the information you've given him and react to it. Give him minimum information at a time. If you bombard him with too much data, he'll nod his head in front of you but later he'll get confused. Finally he'll end up doing the job wrong."

"But we are giving him drawings for his record. The drawing is a ready reference for him, site explanation of the drawing is just for additional clarifications,"Rachna defended her stance.

"Even though you have given a perfect drawing to the contractors, on-site explanation is mandatory. A proper clearance given on site gives them the confidence to proceed with the work. They understand spoken instructions better. It's human tendency. You have textbooks in school containing all studying material but when a teacher explains it to you, it's easier to grasp it. Also, like a teacher re-writes the textbook information on the blackboard, sketches done on site become helpful to convey your thoughts to the contractor." I explained to Rachna with an example.

"Fine I'll work on it," Rachna conceded.

Then I gave her a few final tips, "Remember two most important things while explaining your designs on site. One, keep your vocabulary simple. Your vocabulary should not require explanation. He might not have a dictionary on site. Two, explain the design to him like you would teach a "six-year old". That is very necessary. Don't give the laborer's intellect more credit than that."

Rachna tried very hard to improve on this part of communication, but to this day, it is one aspect which remains yet to be mastered by her one hundred percent.

I mentioned earlier that a client's covenant is to create queries which we, as designers, are expected to resolve. Being in India, the best example to explain this is through cricket. Clients are like different bowlers who bowl fast balls, spinners, Yorkers, wide balls and even no balls. We, in order to defend our stumps, have to aim for a four or a six on every ball, and at least secure a single or two runs. But once in a while comes a ball which catches you off guard and you get stumped. Vijendra Bhatia stumped us.

Vijendra Bhatia's site was handled by Team A - Rachna and Aaisha. For every site, I ensured that clients cleared their dues as per the payment schedules given to them at the start of the project. Failure to do so resulted in slowing the pace of work and even non-progress of work until previous dues were cleared. Vijendra had always stuck to the agreed schedule. It was towards the completion of the site that Anagha, Shirin and I were scheduled for a family vacation to Hyderabad and Ramoji Film City. The designs were finalized and the last bit of execution remained, which Team A was supposed to complete. In return, Vijendra was supposed to hand over the payment installment to Rachna. One evening, Vijendra called Rachna, literally weeping over the phone, expressing grief on the slow progress of work. Rachna explained that she was awaiting payments from him, but his lament knew no end. By now she was used to handling difficult clients, egoistic clients, even ignorant and adamant clients, but she had never handled a crying client. Rachna called me to seek permission to complete the site work without receiving further payments. Keeping in mind Vijendra's past reputation, I told her to complete the site. After site completion, the weeping lamb turned into a roaring tiger and even after much persuasion,Vijendra Bhatia failed to clear our dues. Rachna's faith in clients was redefined. Now, the client's first covenant was to pay up on time. Of course, being humane ensures we still get stumped once a while, even to this day. But every time it happens, we promise ourselves that it'll be the last time and we strive harder towards keeping our promise.

Every day of everyone's life is a learning experience and real growth occurs when you become a little better today than you were yesterday. Growth can be either professional or personal. According to me, learning something new is growth, acquiring the confidence of your colleagues is growth, making a new friend is growth and becoming richer is also growth. Although a little daily growth in everyone, goes unnoticed, when you reflect upon the cumulative result over the years, you remember a few memorable incidents which shaped you.

These are some of the memories I reflected upon, as I paused for a while to cherish this part of my journey down the memory lane.

Fall of a Pillar 6

Palak, Devika and Rachna's friendship grew stronger over time and they would spend hours together even outside office. They went out for coffee and even met on weekends. Aisha, with her ego and insecurity, could never adhere to their group, gradually growing more and more distant. She had frequent arguments and clashes with the three of them and eventually maintained only a minimalistic, professional relationship with them. Her insecurity affected her work output and the stress was evident in the basic nature of the mistakes she made.

Rajesh, on the other hand, refrained from actively participating in most of these events. He always had some pretext to avoid them. He could sense the growing strength of the girls overshadowing his position in the firm, but he put up a brave front. I, on the other hand, could sense his anxiety, since I had mentored him from an early age. I had personally nurtured him and seen him grow as a professional. The insecurity creeping into him did not elude me. I knew that the best way to help him maintain his sanity would be to change his job profile. Hence, I chalked out a new designation for him. I promoted him from a site supervisor to a business developer. It was a diversion from the technical side, which Rajesh was comfortable handling, but with training I knew he would do well. This new vertical was not only the next logical step in the firm's evolution, but also a distraction to reduce Rajesh's interaction with the girls. Although they would be in the same office, they would be working in different departments and therefore, they would seldom interfere in each other's job. Eventually, it would vent out the mounting frustration in the office due to their frequent friction.

I started training Rajesh in the field of marketing, acquiring alliances, sourcing database and other methods of generating leads to enhance the growing business. As I mentioned earlier, intellectual growth for every ambitious individual is as important as the monetary growth. Since Rajesh was ambitious, he had a penchant for this new learning. Rajesh showed interest in the new profile and slowly restricted his site interaction to contractor finalization and crisis management. He avoided day-to-day involvement with site work and only reviewed the site at a macro level. This gave him ample time to concentrate on business development with great enthusiasm and passion. The new profile completed his training in all aspects of the business, except of course designing and client interaction. But, Rajesh never wholly understood the importance of both of these in our business. Alas, the significance of aesthetics and soft skills eluded him. But owing to his experience and seniority, he was still occupying the topmost position in the firm. His decision in any site-related matter was still considered final.

I closely monitored Rajesh's growth as a business developer and was happy with his progress. His experience in sales generation had grown to a stage where he could independently explore new markets. The only problem was that his growth in Pune would be restricted owing to his inability to communicate fluently in English. I reckoned that he would be the ideal candidate to start an office in the growing satellite town Nashik, where Marathi - the local language - was predominant. But, Nashik was a small town and I wasn't sure whether Rajesh would be willing to shift there.

"I think," I interrupted Rajesh as he was discussing some of the recent leads he had generated, "we should start an office in Nashik." Rajesh startled, as I continued, "I have been reading in papers about the extensive development in Nashik and about its potential to become the new IT hub. There is already a real estate boom in Nashik and interior designing will flourish there. How about opening an office in Nashik?"

"Even I heard it come up," Rajesh spoke, as I mentally reconstructed the grammatically incorrect sentences in my head. "I have uncle and aunts there. They tell me to come and meet."

"I have been doing my own research and study. It is an upcoming town and will prove to be an excellent market. Also, Anagha's uncle has a vacant office which we can lease. We will have to renovate it lavishly though. We'll need a good office for clients to visit."

"Who will sit and manage there?" Rajesh questioned.

"I will incur the entire cost for infrastructure, but we need a trustworthy and experienced manager there." Then I asked hesitatingly, "How about you shifting to Nashik?"

A long pause followed, where Rajesh was thinking of the proposal and I was giving him ample time to think. I was reading his facial expressions to check for glimpses of a positive answer. I looking for an affirmative answer because at this stage it seemed best for him to shift.

"Sorry I can't handle so much. How to manage design and clients there? I can't do it." Rajesh replied.

"You won't face any problems," I reassured him. "Dcsigning will be done at Pune. You can email the measurement drawings, the complete designing will be done here and emailed back to you." I spoke encouragingly. "Nashik is only four hours away from here. Sites there could be easily monitored from here."

"And who speak to clients all the time? Sorry, I can't speak to them," he said.

I spoke assertively, "Two days a week, let's fix it on Thursdays and Fridays, I'll visit Nashik to meet up with any new clients. Also, in my spare time I will make site visits on our ongoing projects in Nashik. You consider that practically one-third of my week will be in Nashik. You have to just line up activities accordingly."

"Sorry Boss. I don't want to leave Pune. We are doing good here." Rajesh was firm.

I offered Rajesh a lucrative salary package, "If you shift to Nashik, you will get your current salary plus profit sharing in revenues generated from there. All expenses will be mine, including office infrastructure and your accommodation. But a bachelor accommodation. Eventually, build your own team there! No interference from these girls here. You'll be your own boss!"

Finally I struck the right chord and saw the glee in Rajesh's eye that I was hoping for. He concluded that the offer was good. It would take him miles ahead in his career and give him the desired independence in working without shouldering any risks. Trying to hide his excitement, he spoke in a low tone, "Fine I go, but if I don't like there, I come back."

I warned him sternly, "No, Rajesh! I'll require long term commitment! We'll end up spending a lot of money to set up infrastructure in Nashik. Think thoroughly and decide. Go there and survey the place before we make the expenditure. Once you agree to settle there, it'll have to be a very serious decision and you have to stick by it."

"I know the place. I will go there!"

"Are you absolutely sure?"

"Trust me!"

***

Rajesh exhibited a lot of enthusiasm in setting up the Nashik office. Although, it was smaller than the Pune office in size, we ensured that it spoke of the Dessign7 culture and brand. Rajesh got introduced to multiple developers there for client references. They all welcomed a design agency from Pune with open arms. The crème-de-la-crème people of Nashik, who were always used to hiring interior designers from Pune or Mumbai for their dream homes were willing to award their jobs to us. We had the added advantage of having an execution office in their city. It assured them of a better service. Within a few months we bagged a couple of good bungalow projects. We even recruited two engineers to manage the local projects. The entire business expansion was working as strategized and we were creating our market presence in Nashik. I anticipated that we would breakeven on our expenses even sooner than expected. I was happy for Rajesh, Dessign7 and myself.

***

Rajesh's enthusiasm was like a bottle of champagne. The faster the froth rushes out when you pop open a bottle, the sooner it also fizzles out. Rajesh had promised to stay in Nashik for at least five days a week as he wished to be with his family in Pune for the other two days. Gradually, he came down to staying in Nashik for only four days. Then he started taking mid-week breaks. On one occasion he came back to Pune even without seeking my permission. It was only when I inquired with the local staff there, that I realized he wasn't in Nashik. He started to look for excuses to stay back in Pune for most part of the week. Finally I confronted him.

"Rajesh, is there a problem? You don't seem to be focused on Nashik too well." I asked.

"No problem, everything going smooth," Rajesh replied.

"You've not been paying attention to the Nashik office. You are not spending enough time there. Your schedules have become erratic. Last week you came back without even informing me! Are you serious about Nashik or not?" I asked.

"Actually sir, my wife keeps fighting. She doesn't want me to go and stay at Nashik."

I interrupted, "There are fights in every family! People don't abandon careers for that. Once you settle down there, take her with you."

"Even I feel lonely without her," he mumbled.

"What about the projects that we have started there? Aren't they lonely without you?"

"I was going to speak to you about that. I can complete that, but no new projects please. I think I can do better in Pune. Bigger market to explore," Rajesh went on to explain.

I heard him patiently and finally asked, "What about the infrastructure and advertisement expense already made? Who'll bear the loss?"

Rajesh had nothing to say in his defense. I tried to boost his morale in many ways. I tried active and passive counseling; I tried to make the incentives more lucrative; I even showed to him the shining career I had in store for him, but in vain. He had completely lost interest in Nashik office and expressed his final decision to shift back to Pune. Three months later, Rajesh conveniently resumed his earlier position in the office, neglecting the losses incurred. But, I could never forget his words, "Trust me!"

Unfortunately, I had trusted him.

***

In the meantime, the design teams in Pune had fully acquired charge and were completely competent to handle sites without any senior supervision. Also, the contractors were happy with the clarity of drawings that they were receiving. Out of the short listed contractors, both the teams selected the contractors that they were comfortable working with for their sites. This made them accountable for completion of the site on time. Also, to stream line the execution and iron out any lack of clarity between the designers and the clients we had devised a system of getting sign-offs from the clients on all finalized designs. Rajesh was no longer required to look into site execution in Pune.

Rajesh was back in Pune, with a lost focus and will. His lack of enthusiasm was becoming more prominent. He was missing from office for long hours and his lunch breaks usually extended beyond the permissible hour. His disorientation did raise a few fleeting doubts but I flouted them as Rajesh to me was loyalty personified. There was no doubting the untarnished loyalty of the last seven years. I chose to believe that he was disturbed by the debacle of Nashik, and wanted to give him time to recover.

****

Not every sunny morning brings a fine day. Since the beginning of the day I had an instinct that 1st April was going to be a day of pranks in office. I trusted the office staff to be naughty enough to come up with something special. Rahul, our electrical contractor, had asked me to accompany him post lunch for a very important site visit. And he insisted that I would not discuss it with anyone in office. It was an unusual request as generally my site visits were planned upon request of the design staff. I was sure that the girls had organized something for the Fools Day and I was prepared for the fun.

It was a hot summer afternoon, the kind that could deter anyone from stepping outdoors. Since Anagha didn't have a hectic schedule, I asked her to accompany Rahul and myself for the surprise site visit. We had a regular conversation during our drive to the site. Nothing in Rahul's words or expressions betrayed the purpose of our visit. He navigated me to an unknown residential society called Citadel Residency. We had never been there before, so inquiringly Anagha said, "You said we were going for a site visit. We are not doing a project here."

"Is it a new client?" I inquired.

Rahul maintained his silence for a moment and later he answered calmly, "Don't ask questions sir, just follow me."

I parked my car in visitors parking. The three of us went up to the 4th Floor in the elevator and stood in front of a dirty brown door without a nameplate. It was obvious that the flat was under renovation. We entered the house. I saw a few unknown and a few familiar faces of laborers. I looked at Rahul with a puzzled expression and asked, "Why have we come here?"

"The electrical work of this site was offered to me. Before I commence the work on site, I require your permission to take up this project."

"Why would I deny? Whose project is this?" I asked still baffled by the entire chain of events which were unfolding.

"I thought as much that you were unaware of this project. It's our project," Rahul said pointing to the drawing pasted on the wall.

I could see the Dessign7 logo on the drawings, but didn't recognize the drawings. The colors, the lines the entire effects on the drawing were similar to our style of designing but still something was missing. It seemed different in a strange way. It lacked certain finesse which was signatory of Dessign7.

I looked at Anagha and said, "This looks like our drawings with our company name but strangely it is not ours. Some designers is forging our name." Then I turned to Rahul, "Who is this weirdo?"

Rahul said with a sly smile, "I have called the designer also. I told him that I had a few queries and requested him to meet me on site. He should be coming any moment now."

"Stop building the suspense! Do I happen to know the designer?"

Just as I spoke, the door opened and Rajesh walked in. I saw him and spoke, "Rajesh! I am glad you are here. Did you see this? Some designer is using our name to bag jobs. Using our credibility. This is pathetic. Luckily he contacted Rahul for the electrical works and he brought us here. Find out who this is and let's get the police to pursue this. We'll sue him," I blabbered non-stop.

Rajesh stood still for a moment. "Why you get him here?" Rajesh shouted at Rahul.

Rajesh was always protective about me and I knew he couldn't stand me being hurt. I said, "It is OK Rajesh, I can handle it. Rahul in how much time is the culprit coming?"

"He is already here, in front of you."

"Rajesh? Rajesh?" I exclaimed.

Rajesh was crying. "Sir please forgive me! I thought I can handle a few sites with office work," Rajesh was muttering words amidst loud sobs.

I was shocked. I was confused whether the sunny morning had just turned cloudy or was it my head which was spinning. "Rajesh,what a silly fool's day prank. Let's go Anagha, the joke is over!" I said disgusted with the entire episode. Then I added with an afterthought, "Please tell me this is not true."

"I come here during lunch break and after office hours. Not during office timing," Rajesh broke into an explanation.

"Rajesh, I am shattered! The trust I had in you is shattered. You betrayed us. You are aware of the amount of time and effort that Anagha and I have put for your development. Waste, absolute waste. Totally gone down the drain today." I turned to Anagha with tears in my eyes, "He back stabbed us."

Anagha held my hand. She held it tight to reassure me that she was by my side. And I stared at her with questioning eyes, trying to cover up the moisture in my eyes. Finally she asked Rajesh, "Do you know how much it cost to set up the Nashik office? All of it wasted because you weaseled your way back from there."

I continued, "We never asked you to pay for your change of mind. Instead, we still took you back as a part of the Dessign7 family. And this is the way you repay us?" I shouted at the top of my voice.

"I needed a little extra money. Didn't mean to hurt you. I thought,"

I interrupted him, "You bastard! If you needed extra money you should have asked us. We have helped you in the past, would have helped you again."

"For how long would I keep taking your help? I wanted to earn my own money," Rajesh argued.

"So you go ahead and cheat us," Anagha exclaimed.

"How the bloody hell can you do this? I taught business development to you. And you use the same skills to cheat me? Don't you find it ethically wrong, you dog?"

Rajesh tried to justify himself, "I never cheat you. From the clients that I get, all high profile clients I give for Dessign7. All other small budget clients only I keep."

"And you also abused the company name," Anagha said.

I added, "You used our company name and profile to get your clients. The client you are working for thinks he has hired Dessign7, isn't it?"

"Yes," Rajesh mumbled.

"So you've swindled him also. You used our contractors, our strategies and our company name. Disgusting dog. If you wanted to take up work independently, you could have sought my permission. Or you could have left the job, gracefully and done your sites. Then maybe I would have even helped you," I stated, still appalled by the felony.

"I don't want to leave Dessign7. I took small jobs that you not take. So I thought no harm. I am very sorry," Rajesh justified himself shamelessly.

"Was this the reason for disowning Nashik office? And your lack of interest in Dessign7's work?" I was slowly assembling the jigsaw pieces. I shouted, "It was, wasn't it? Answer me damn it!" Rajesh stood there quietly.

By that time, I had lost patience. In a bout of anger, I flung my right fist. I struck his left lower jaw, staggering Rajesh off his feet. Before he could recover, another blow headed for him. From the side, Anagha held my hand and exclaimed, "Don't! Let him go! You'll hurt him and yourself! Just let it go!"

I freed my hand. I didn't want to harm Rajesh further, but the anger within me was frustrating. I looked around for something on which I could vent out my anger. I caught sight of a box of tiles lying in the corner. I walked over and swung my fist right on to the box, shattering the tiles in half. A few splinters flew and the next thing I saw was blood dripping down my palm. Rajesh rushed from behind, shouting "Sir don't break tiles, I will face loss! They are expensive."

Anagha quickly strode towards me. She held my hand. She saw the blood dripping. She wiped some of it and placed her handkerchief on the wound. She ushered me off site, giving Rajesh a livid stare and mumbling a few abuses. A long silence followed as we left his site. I recalled Rajesh's words, "Trust me!" Unfortunately, I had trusted him.

I immediately decided to sack Rajesh from the job. Rajesh could no longer be a part of Dessign7. I returned to office, walked into the studio and standing near Rajesh's empty cubicle, I announced to all,

"Rajesh is no longer working with us!"

"Sir we know it's 1st of April," Rachna smiled, and suddenly paused. Her smile slowly changed to a frown as she noticed the blood dripping down my hand. "Are you serious?"

I was serious. Rajesh was not coming back to Dessign7. I maintained a strong front,but emotionally, I was shattered. I recalled the tile breaking incident from earlier that day. Rajesh was more concerned about the cost of the tiles than blood flowing from my hand. I was hurt and in tears. Rajesh had been with Dessign7 since its inception. I couldn't fathom its future it without him. After a lot of discussion that evening, my conclusive statement to Anagha was, "Pay Rajesh the money for the damaged tiles. Let him go and find his way, hopefully he will also seek his soul. As for us, guess we just have to fight a little harder!"

7 The Offer

April fool's day had taught me a lot. I learned that no one is indispensable in life. Growth is the natural evolution of any living being. The vacuum created by Rajesh was not going to be filled soon, especially when I had four competent designers, none of whom could be individually promoted without hurting the other egos. Therefore, we continued with a flat organization.

The fun and frolic was still a part of our regular day. Devika's sudden inclination to latest fad of power yoga had its effect on us as well. It made us all look up to her as a health guru. After a hectic day of work, the office doors were locked and the studio was converted into a yoga hall. Devika exercised her authority and under her guidance we all exercised, some to reduce fat and some to become fit. As for me, I did it to avoid being a spoil sport. Everyone looked forward to the evenings, when Devika would start her workout sessions. She had devised special amateur exercise for all of us, knowing that all of us were neither fit nor agile. Each set of exercise was assigned a count. Based on the number of the counts assigned, the particular exercise had to be repeated to complete the set. Any defaulter, usually me, would result in stagnated counting for everyone and repeated calls of the same numbers over and over again till the defaulter would catch pace. Stagnated counting was a technique devised by her to make us do additional sets of exercise without actually giving us the credit of doing those additional sets. We all hated Devika's mathematics skills.

Palak and Devika, along with being teammates, were also 'gym pals'. They worked out together in the same gym every morning and usually went together on the same bike. It was one such Wednesday morning when both of them surprised me by being extremely late for work. Even their phones were switched off. What was unusual was that even Rachna couldn't trace them and was extremely worried herself. It was unlike them to be late without prior intimation. They were unreachable, which had us worried, until Rachna managed to get in touch with Devika,

"Where are you? We are all worried, no call, no message, what happened? Is Palak with you? Even she's not answering her phone." Rachna questioned rapidly.

"Palak is with me. We are at the hospital," Devika spoke softly.

"What? Where? Why?" Rachna asked. She could feel the tremor in her voice.

"It happened in the morning, whilst we were on our way back from the gym, we met with an accident. A bloody bike guy recklessly broke the signal and banged into the side of my bike. Palak was sitting behind. He rammed the bike right into her leg. I just got a few minor scratches on my arms and legs; also nothing much has happened to the bike but…." Devika gave a long dramatic pause.

"Devika, what happened? Tell me what happened!" Rachna asked, cupping her fingers to imply the question.

"Palak, unfortunately, fractured her toes and severely sprained her ankle," Devika stammered, "I have brought her to Jehangir Hospital and the doctors said they will have to operate on her toes. I've called her mother; she's on her way. I am shit worried, it really wasn't my fault…"

"Don't worry! You calm down, I'll inform sir and come right there. Once I reach Jehangir, I'll give you a call," was Rachna's closing remark. Rachna informed me of the morning's event and hurried to the hospital.

Anagha and I visited Palak once she was back home. Her condition was severe; she was advised a month's bed rest, but she assured us she would join back after that. However, owing to her condition she was out of office for a month.

***

Meanwhile, after a sour breakup with her childhood sweetheart, Aaishawas going through an emotional crisis. Her focus on work had diminished drastically. She was having a burnout syndrome, and errors at a basic level were causing losses of time, money and sometimes reputation. She was beginning to notice her own absent-mindedness and began losing confidence. The slip-up in the Bank of Baroda project was the last straw that broke the camel's back.

Aaisha had assisted me for all of the six Bank of Baroda branches that we had designed and executed to date, making her an expert in understanding their design, documentation and procedural requirements. As their empanelled consultants, we had recently finished designing their M.G. Road branch in Pune and the tender for the fit-out had to be submitted online for e-bidding by other registered contractors. Aaisha and I jointly prepared the final tender and it was her job to upload it – a procedure she had already done four times previously. Aaisha completed the task. I asked her to inform the same to the Premise and Estate Manager of the bank, to enable him to start the e-bidding process. The tenders went live. As per the bank's guidelines, a pre-bid meeting was arranged a week later. The purpose of this meeting was to give the contractors an opportunity to clarify any queries regarding the tender. Aaisha and I chaired the meeting and were confused by the absurd queries we received. The queries were regarding works not even listed in the tender we had prepared. To be entirely sure, I examined the uploaded copy of the tender. I compared it with our office copy. I was confounded. It was immediately clear that the error was on our end. I realized that Aaisha had uploaded the wrong tender.

All hell broke loose in office that day. I was so angry and frustrated that I broke into a fit of laughter. A very angry, sarcastic rage of laughter. No one in the office had seen me laugh like that before. Rachna later confessed as one of her scariest moments in Dessign7. I eventually pardoned the mistake, but Aaisha couldn't forgive herself. Towards the end of May, she submitted her resignation. Even after much persuasion and asking her to join back after a sabbatical, she remained firm on her decision to resign. She had decided to pursue further education in the field of Interior Project Management. I asked her to stay on for a month and complete the sites that she was currently handling and she obliged.

***

Rachna had a very different problem playing in her mind. Disha, Rachna's elder sister, was going to get married soon and Rachna wanted to buy her an expensive, designer, wedding dress with her own hard earned money. A gift that Disha would always remember and cherish. Rachna selected the ideal dress well in advance designed by a prominent designer in Pune. She knew that she would have to shell out a handsome price for it and therefore she started saving money for it. The D-day was approaching fast but her bank balance was not matching up to the desired figure. No extent of adjustment in expenditure was allowing her to reach her goal. Finally she gave up and her parent's bought the dress for Disha. But, Rachna was dejected and sad. She was frustrated that her salary wasn't sufficient to support her wish. She wasn't the kind of person who prioritized money, but this incident jolted her. She felt that she deserved a raise but she had never discussed her salary with me since the time she joined Dessign7. She never felt the need to before that day. She thought and evaluated the entire situation in depth and finally mustered enough courage to discuss the topic with me. The following week Rachna approached me in my cabin.

"Sir, I would like to discuss something with you," Rachna sought permission to begin the dialogue, "Is this a good time?"

"Tell me," I said, looking towards her. I knew that any conversation that began with 'I want to discuss something' could never impart good news.

"I am sorry for being so direct, but I needed to tell you this," Rachna continued with intermittent pauses. "I have been working here for over three years now and I was hoping to get a raise. Fuel and other expenses have gone up and it's difficult to adjust within the current salary."

I heard the explanation and silently wondered whether any of our clients would sanction an additional budget for their projects if I told them about the recent fuel hike. I smiled to myself for a moment and returned to our conversation. I wasn't the kind of person who would procrastinate in announcing a decision I had already taken, so I explained the situation to Rachna, "I understand where you are coming from, but going by the current scenario, I will not be able to increase your pay. You see, when we moved from a salary model to a salary plus incentive model, all four of you were aware that it factored for your travel and phone bills. Also, all four of you are at par and I can't increase just your salary; the raise will have to be for everyone, which we can't afford at the moment. Your salaries and incentives form the major part of a project's overhead cost. Let me illustrate it for you." I went on to explain to her the profit calculation of each site and that the basic salary plus profit-sharing incentive being paid to them already stretched the calculated overheads.

Rachna had a good mind for numbers and I knew she understood the math, but her decision was final. "Sir, I understand. I appreciate everything that you have taught me but it will be difficult for me to continue." She paused waiting for my reaction. She gave a slight smile and said, "I would like to resign."

"Do you have any other offer in hand?" I enquired.

"No, not at all. I haven't even given it a thought. I was thinking of taking a short break once I leave. The past few months at work have been hectic and I think I deserve a break." She spoke frankly.

"Will you at least manage to complete the sites you have in hand?" I asked her, although I was sure that she understood her responsibility well and would never leave anyone in a lurch.

"Yes, of course. I'll complete the projects I am working on." She smiled graciously, with a little disappointment in her eyes.

As she got up from her seat, I asked her a final question, "Is salary the only reason for resigning?"

"Yes sir, otherwise it's been a pleasure working for you," she concluded. The next day she left her resignation on my table, effective immediately after completion of sites in hand.

****

Palak was back from her medical leave and didn't seem to enjoy work as much as she previously did. It soon dawned upon her that she was bored of the present job and desired a career change. Also, knowing the fact that Rachna had already resigned did aggravate these feelings. She chose to resign as well. I explained to her that eventually challenge ceases in every job and monotony creeps in.

"Sir, it's not really that I am bored," Palak started with her narration, "but I don't want to do the same thing. See, designing is good. It's nice, creative, satisfying and I like it. But contracting isn't. I don't like to follow-up with laborers every day to ensure that they get done with their daily tasks. I don't think that's my passion."

"So, you planning to join a firm that'll do only designing? You think you'll not have to follow up with contractors there?" I asked.

"No. I think I am done with interior designing and would like to explore some other field. Something more creative and artistic." Palak added after a pause, "May be writing or journalism? Not sure."

"You know Palak, today age is on your side and that will work to your advantage in any career you choose. But that'll not always remain the case. So, if today you want a change of career, it is okay, but introspect and decide upon the profession you are inclined to and stick to that. You can't keep making career shifts too often."

"I understand and appreciate your advice sir. Will bear that in mind."

"Good Luck and enjoy life!"

Palak was beyond reasoning and her mind was made up. Hence,I also accepted her resignation.

The finale of this stressful episode was Devika's resignation. Devika walked in with her resignation stating that she wanted to join her fiancé,Shahnawaz in his business. He was a practicing interior designer and an esteemed junior of mine. Devika was not a girl of many words and her decision was announced to me softly but firmly. Also, I agreed with her reason for leaving. Just like Anagha had always supported me in business since its inception, it seemed only fair for Devika to extend the same support to Shahnawaz. Since there was no scope of reasoning, without any resistance or explanation, I accepted her resignation as well.

Although the reasons for all the resignations differed, their timing was in perfect synchrony, which made me feel like a victim of conspiracy. Rajesh's betrayal was still fresh in my mind and I felt that the cycle of infidelity was repeating again. After sacking Rajesh in April, to an empty studio by the end of June, I had only a few days to revive our design studio – the backbone of our office. The task was mammoth even for Anagha and me to manage, but my survival instinct kicked in.

I analyzed the individual reasons for all the resignations. Aaisha was over-saturated with work but her pressure would vent if the other three left. Maybe she could rebound to her earlier spirit. Also, she respected me enough to stay on for a few months, if persuaded. But, I wasn't sure if the burnout syndrome would appear again the next time someone more efficient walked in. Next, we had Palak, who was bored with her job, seeking new challenge. But every challenge would eventually fizzle out and inevitably boredom would step in. Also, she wasn't tough enough to deal with contractors permanently. Asking Devika to stay on didn't even cross my mind. Rachna was the only one who was passionate about continuing with Dessign7 provided she had constant growth in work, learning and remuneration. So finally,if colleagues on par with Rachna resigned, I could promote her to look after a fresh design team. I truly believed that she had the capability to manage a design team on her own and was confident that she would willingly accept the challenge.

At the next available opportunity I spoke to Rachna, "You obviously know that even Palak, Devika and Aaisha have resigned?"She nodded. "Don't resign now," I said, "Hold on to your resignation for a month. Let the others leave and I'll make you an offer you can't refuse." Rachna obliged and waited for a month.

At the end of the month, I sought a clarification from Rachna, "Before I discuss my offer, I wanted to ask you something. Why did you all resign together in the same month?"

"I didn't understand the question."

"Why were all your resignations planned in the last month?"

"It wasn't planned, it was an accident. When I spoke to you about my resignation, I didn't even know about the others." She continued in an attempt to ensure I understood her completely, "It wasn't a conspiracy or something. We wouldn't dare to do something like that to you. We all respect you far too much for us to even contemplate a scheme against you."

"I was quite shocked with the coincidence."

"I am sorry if it appeared planned, but it wasn't. All of us will always support you if you ever need it. I can confidently speak for all of us."

"Glad to hear that, anyways coming to the agenda," I proceeded to make my offer to Rachna.

"I know you are unhappy about your salary but a month ago, an increment was not possible. The four of you had always been on par, and with your colleagues still onboard, I couldn't raise only your salary. It wouldn't be fair to the others. But now that they have left, I would like to offer you a three point power packed proposal which I am sure you will not refuse. So here it goes.

"One – You will get a collective profit-sharing incentive of all the sites we do. This will shoot up your salary to almost three times as compared to your current salary!" I stressed on the words 'three times' to create the right impact.

"Two – You'll be designated as the Design Head. You can have your own team of junior designers and site supervisors. You can decide on the number of juniors you require. You can decide on their pre-requisite qualifications and experience. You can interview candidates, recruit the ones you select, and train them to suit your way of working." This time my voice stressed on all the 'Yours'.

"Three – As the Design Head, you will have the ultimate verdict in finalizing the designs for any site. No overruling even by me! You will get the complete opportunity to explore your creativity." 'Ultimate verdict' were the keywords in the last point. Rachna was absorbing the proposal and whilst I was giving her time to think, I was constantly gauging her reaction. A long pause followed, after which I finally spoke again.

"Frankly Rachna, after the kind of learning, exposure and creative freedom that you have gained here, I don't think that you'll be able to easily accommodate yourself into any other organization, especially in a junior position. And, with less than three years of experience, you will not be eligible for a managerial position. So, the only available option with you is to start your own design studio, which I am positive will be a big success eventually. But the question is what about now? What about the present? When I left Ar. Amala Sheth, I realized one thing. Starting your own business throws you down to the bottom of the chain, where the scale and size of the assignments you get are minuscule. The projects at that level are small in size with meagre budgets. Such clients neither appreciate your creativity and nor do they have the budgets to fulfill your whims and fancies. And it takes a lot of time and effort to work your way to the top.

"Also, keep in mind that starting your own office means you'll have to incur a lot of office expenses. You'll be required to invest in an office space; staff expenses and salaries are high; computers and software cost a bomb; and maintaining all these is a totally different ball game. It's for you to decide whether the entire effort of setting up your own practice is worthwhile, or whether it is easier to stay with Dessign7, where you focus on designing and site execution and we focus on improvement and expansion of the organization. Let's grow together.

"Think wise and think fast. It's a good opportunity to comeback. The sky is now your limit." I concluded, giving Rachna a realistic insight into the business of interior designing.

Rachna was continuously evaluating the proposal, whilst I was bombarding her with information to demotivate her from leaving the job. Images of her already planned vacation - post her early retirement from Dessign7 - were flashing through her mind. She was looking forward to a break after three long and hectic years in Dessign7. On the other hand, this would provide her with an opportunity to almost own a design studio with unlimited growth in creativity and remuneration - an opportunity which would not definitely revisit her in the near future. The dilemma on her face was evident but I didn't want to influence her any further. I wanted her to absorb the offer, evaluate it and make a sound decision based on the merits of the offer. A hasty decision at this time would only spell regret later.

Rachna wanted to continue in Dessign7 but had the luxury of holding back her answer on the pretext of evaluating the offer. I, on the other hand, was an impatient person who never walked off a negotiating table before sealing the deal. I could see that Rachna needed a little help in deciding, so I played my trump card, "You realize, of course, that if you accept the offer, you'll occupy the coveted cubicle which is vacant since the time Rajesh left."

After careful evaluation, Rachna answered.

***

It was sometime in the last week of June, a very regular day with only work and stress to look forward to, when Rachna walked into the office and Zeenat greeted her with her usual pleasant "Good morning, Ma'am". Rachna, with all her capabilities and foresight, had made the right decision. She earned her position as the Design Head of Dessign7, the first ever position truly created for any employee. Almost three years after she joined Dessign7, the glorious years of fun had evolved into the "The Growing Years". A journey of growth had begun for all - for Rachna, for us, and for Dessign7.

Dawn of an Era 8

"On the journey towards growth, it's easy to constantly march ahead, but it takes courage to leap towards success, especially when fate is making efforts to push you a few steps back." I started a new chapter in Rachna's life with motivational philosophy. "Fate has taken us back. Now let's plan our leap."

****

Rachna walked into the studio with a senior position, where ironically, there were no juniors. The entire staff had left with only the new core team of Rachna, Anagha and I. The strange coincidence was that the initials of the core team were still the same; only Rajesh had been replaced by Rachna. She was less daring and less bold than him, but was more cultured, well-spoken and had finesse. What set her apart drastically were her core moral values and ethics.

The evolution for her was going to be a tough one. Three years of field experience had restricted her growth to the technical side of interior designing only. The challenge now was to multiply the hours in a day; to train others to fill the vacuum in the studio; and to manage junior interior designers.

Rachna had to undergo a metamorphosis to become a manager,just like a caterpillar transforms into a butterfly. As a fresh graduate from a college, she was like a caterpillar which had hatched out into the industry. She was hungry for information. She fed upon all information available, endlessly until she became a perfect technician. Technically, she had the ability to understand and complete any task. She could survive through adverse situations. But the caterpillar had fed on sufficient information. Now it was time to develop further. She was within her cocoon as a technician and she had to break-free from that to adopt new methods of working. Breaking free from the cocoon was not only essential for the purpose of completing her own growth cycle, but also for soaring high, for acquiring new colors of life and for becoming complete - a complete entrepreneur. Rachna had to break the cocoon. She had to accept the challenge. She had to become "the butterfly".

We started outlining our strategy. "Your immediate task is to get control of all sites in progress," I advised Rachna. "First, get in touch with all the girls and ask them for updates on any dialogues that they have had with their respective clients. Make a list of pending decision, if any. Second, go through all the minutes of the meetings in every file; ask the contractors for any instructions issued on site and verify them from the girls respectively; and last but not the least, introduce yourself to all clients as the new Design Head."I silently smiled as I saw Rachna beam at the last statement.

"Palak was anyway away for a long time because of her accident and sites that I was working on with Aaisha, I am well aware of. Let me check with Devika for her inputs," Rachna added, as she made her phone call to Devika. Devika's friendship and loyalty were qualities I'll never forget. She extended maximum support to Rachna to complete the sites she was working on. She even made site visits to ensure work was progressing smoothly. For all other sites, though Rachna thought it was easy, there were lots of minor details that she had to iron out. A recap of client discussions was essential to learn any deviations from the drawings that were executed on site. A feedback from the contractors for the pending decisions was mandatory to update the list of details to be furnished on site. She needed to transform herself into a Hindu goddess with five pairs of hands, juggling multiple responsibilities. There was a lot of work to do and very little time. Of course, I was there to help her, but the struggle was hers. A systematic evolution was required.

Rachna was technically strong and business communication was her forte, so within a short span of time, the sites were organized, streamlined, and functioning as per our expectation. But she was handicapped for time. Without any juniors to off load some part of her responsibilities, it was becoming more and more challenging to cope with the ever-increasing workload. There was a strong need for interior designing staff.

***

Evolution is the process of transformation in an organism or organization which equips it to adapt to the changing environment. It was not so much for me, but for Rachna that the environment had changed, along with the change in role, authority and power. I quoted to her from the movie Spiderman, "With great power comes great responsibility, this is your blessing, this is your curse."

She had just got a grasp of sites in hand, which was anenormous expansion of her previous profile, but her first step to evolution had yet to commence. The initiation came when she demanded juniors to cope with the existing work load, "Sir, we'll need to recruit fresh talent."

"Good. So go ahead and do it," I smiled.

"How do I do it? I was hoping you'd help me out," Rachna emphasized on the word 'you', expressing her lack of experience for the task.

"You tell me. If you were looking for juniors where would you start looking?"

"I don't know. Typically give an ad in the papers or register on various job portals for junior interior designers."

"Think of an easier avenue. When you started looking for a job, whom did you first contact?"

"The institute's placement cell."

"So contact various design institutes and speak to their placement cell."I put the ball back in her court. I always enjoyed a unique way of teaching where I never believed in answering the question, but always assisted the student to self-seek the solutions. The answers are always available within;one only requires the right guidance to recognize them.

She took guidance and assistance from Anagha, and they contacted various training institutes for fresh graduates and experienced candidates willing to work with us. We interviewed all sorts of candidates: tall ones and short ones, boys and girls, fresher and experienced ones, but could not find smart and dedicated ones. It just reiterated the fact that HR guys are still demigods. Enlightened about the fact that "The Glorious Years" of Dessign7 were not coming back soon, we settled for the four best candidates available to us to fill life into the deserted studio.

Rachna trained the new staff to assist her in drafting designs and site execution. Independent tasks were given and continual assessments were made to look for a spark of dedication - the spark which encourages better teaching; to take extra efforts to train; to pay more attention to queries; to respect opinions. We were looking for a fourth pillar of support.

Training someone always has dual effects. It not only educates the student, but also trains the trainer. Different ways of teaching the same thing have to be derived to teach different students, in order to connect well with each of them. This attempt to connect with different people also helps entrepreneurs to sub-consciously develop their interaction skills with clients.

The employees, trained by Rachna, showed a lot of respect for her, but their loyalty to the firm was missing. It was the typical frog mentality of the younger lot, who preferred to job-hop for a better salary instead of focusing on developing their own abilities to perform better. The new staff was floating, with a high level of attrition. There was an absolute lack of dedication and sincerity within them, which contrasted the work culture that we had established. Rachna was struggling to get good quality designs and drawings from the fresher lot, but in vain. The workload was ever increasing and high-profile clients demanded classier designs. We strived hard to keep pace.

****

"Rachna, make a 3D view of the entire room," demanded Zarine Khan unreasonably, unaware that her decision to make a 3D view at this stage would delay the stringent schedule of project completion and would add up to the designing costs. "It'll help me visualize the room better."

Zarine was the CEO of a leading software company, making her a very demanding client. I think all CEOs are demanding clients, because in the process of reaching the zenith of success, they acquire the art of extracting the best from others. Rachna had to convince Zarine against the 3D view without hurting her ego. Rachna pacified her, "If you insist, we can create a 3D view, but it'll unnecessarily delay the work and it'll also add to your costs." After a short pause she continued, "Actually you have superb visualization. I am quite surprised that you are having difficulty envisaging it. Let's start from the initial planning stage and I'll run you through the entire concept again. I am sure you'll be able to picture it." Rachna explained all room designs starting from the initial layouts, to design philosophy to concepts and design specifics, until Zarine finally understood, satisfactorily visualized, and gave her approval.

Rachna's patience with people had increased. She was developing the ability to manage clients from different socio-economic backgrounds. She was learning the art of reading between the lines when a client briefed her about their requirements. She was connecting with them.

****

Vaishali was an interior design graduate, who had joined us as a trainee. Although she was a fresher with no field experience, she was a dedicated learner and a smart worker. She followed instructions meticulously and eventually contributed to the designs with her own creative suggestions. Rachna finally spotted the desired spark of commitment in Vaishali. She spent long, sincere hours training Vaishali on the technical intricacies of designing and site supervision. Besides being a good learner, Vaishali confidently accepted Rachna as her mentor and was growing to be her dedicated student. Vaishali reminded me of Rachna's early days. Her respect and loyalty was evident by the delightful surprise she planned.

It was Teacher's Day – 5th September 2010. Shirin had a special recital in her school to celebrate the occasion. Since parents were invited for the celebration, Anagha and I attended the event in the morning. We picked up Shirin after the function and reached our office in the afternoon. Shortly after we arrived, Rachna and the rest of the staff walked into the cabin with the expected surprise – a bouquet and a cake from Rachna, to continue the office tradition. The unexpected surprise came when Vaishali followed her in, with an additional bouquet and cake. As she placed the cake on the table in front of me, Rachna, a little startled, lifted the cover off the second cake and read the words on the yellow wafer biscuit, "Happy Teacher's Day to Rachna Ma'am". Rachna was so spellbound that words couldn't convey her feelings. A smile on her face and a pair of moist eyes conveyed her feelings. A tight hug from Rachna to Vaishali completed the picture-perfect scene. We cut two cakes in the office that day. Ever since Teacher's Day celebrations in office had been upgraded forever. Life had completed a full circle with the student now becoming the teacher.

Rachna had established her authority in Dessign7. The younger brigade of designers looked up to her as their mentor. She had finally managed to build her own design team.

But any team is always vulnerable. Besides job satisfaction, there could be various reasons for employee attrition – shifting to another city, opting fora better job prospect, egoistic clashes between colleagues or merely boredom in the job. Previously, I had faced the brunt of employee attrition and gone through the struggle of building a new team multiple times. It was the struggle to find the right support staff that made me realize the need for a second level of evolution. I was looking for ways and means to be less dependent on human efficiency, hence becoming more system driven. I believed that if systems were strengthened, then the three-member core team of Dessign7 could smoothly monitor a larger number of projects with the assistance of our constantly changing junior staff. I consulted friends and colleagues for an ideal solution. My search finally ended with Quality Management Systems.

****

Quality Management System (QMS) was the ideal solution to the problem we had at hand. More popularly known as ISO certification, I believed that implementation of the same would reduce our dependency on staff and improve communication with clients and contractors. Also, standardizing procedures would help to teach the working style of the firm to any newly-appointed staff. But the challenge was that I had never come across a design firm with standardization.

Theoretically, a design firm is supposed to have a creative expression and create a unique design solution for every project. Every client has an individual, unique requirement and, therefore, each design solution has to be unique. I discussed this idea with Anagha and Rachna to get their view on it. After a thorough brainstorming session we questioned the conventional norm itself, "Does every client have a unique requirement?" A client comes to us wanting a comfortable, cozy and low-maintenance home; rarely a designer masterpiece. Also standardization of procedure would not compromise on creativity. It would lay down a sequential process to be followed from inception to completion of a site and ensure that all communication exchanged with clients is well documented for any future reference. And so the decision to implement the QMS was taken. Dessign7 would be ISO certified.

****

Mr. Kulkarni was a straight-faced man, fairly well-built with a neatly trimmed moustache, who rarely smiled. He was appointed by the auditing firm to train us on the procedure of QMS and to guide us inpreparing our very own Quality Manual. His stern appearance and habit to sport a sarcastic grin whenever he knew something more than us made him the perfect trainer. Anagha, Rachna and I spent long, early morning hours in training with him, well before the day got busy with the routine,hectic work. Rachna's contribution mainly came for the design and site execution processes, which was the crux of our business. She divided and sub-divided the design and site execution process into various milestones which could easily be monitored. All the clients were assigned a file number and there was a minimum set of documentation which formed the skeleton of each file. Every client decision, along with all client approvals and requests for changes, were to be recorded in a prescribed format. Forms were prepared to record data given by the client and checklists were prepared to ensure qualitative implementation of designs on site. Commencement and completion certificates were introduced to earmark the beginning and end of every site. Clients were introduced to various stages of approvals without which we would not proceed to the next level of designing. Payments terms were linked to the approval of every stage of designing and implementation. Flowcharts were prepared to record working processes and bar charts to record the time devoted to execute every site. Even the marketing, sales, admin and HR formats were devised and implemented along with a vision statement for the firm. All of this was to become a part of our Quality Manual.

"Good work everyone," Mr. Kulkarni genuinely smiled, pleased with the completion of our training period. "We have done very well and it was a pleasure to work with all of you. We will have our Initial Audit next week. The audit will last an entire day. The auditors will be here, at your office, by 10:30. You'll have an opening meeting during which they will brief you on the agenda for the day. The detailed agenda will be mailed to you. Before lunch, during the first half of the day they will audit the files and records in office to ensure that they are maintained in accordance with the Quality Manual. They will conduct random checks, so ensure the complete filling system is updated. Also, since this is your first audit, they will expect you to thoroughly know the Quality Manual, especially the Quality Policy. Instruct the complete staff to memorize the Quality Policy! It is very important! Post lunch, they'll conduct a site inspection of any one of the sites you choose. Choose a site where substantial work has been carried out. Ensure that the relevant drawing files and documentation is readily available on site as well. In the evening, there will be a closing meeting. The auditors will share their reports with you. They'll highlight any major or minor non-conformities with you which will have to be rectified before the next audit. So, that's it and best of luck," he wished us, as he removed a book from his brown leather bag and placed it on the table in front of us. After almost three months of training, we looked at our final bound copy of the Quality Manual and we were pleased at the documentation of our new and improved business process. We had managed to document our business synopsis in the Quality Manual. We were very excited for the new way of working and although it appeared exhaustive initially, we could foresee the benefits of this evolution. Of the three of us, Anagha most understood the importance of QMS implementation because she had started her career with a large ISO certified corporate.

"So, before I take your leave, any questions?" asked Mr. Kulkarni.

"What are non-conformities?" asked Rachna.

"Well, if they observe that you are not following a particular part of the QMS, they'll record it as non-conformity. If it's a small error, for example, the index sheet in the file is missing then that is a minor non-conformity. If you have completely skipped one of the procedures, for example, you have not conducted any development trainings at all during the year then it's recorded as a major non-conformity. Minor non-conformities are recorded and are to be rectified by you before the next audit, but a major non-conformity will result in you losing the ISO Certification. Besides these, the auditors can also suggest non-mandatory changes for improving the company's process. Like I said, these are non-mandatory. So you may or may not incorporate them before the next audit. I hope it answers your question, Ms. Vora," answered Mr. Kulkarni with a smile.

"And how many non-conformities are allowed in an audit, ensuring that we still clear the audit?" was my immediate next question.

"You want to know what the passing marks are. Well, it is subjective, depending upon the auditor and how serious he finds a non-conformity. Anything else?" Mr. Kulkarni questioned, but the smile had disappeared.

"Mr. Kulkarni, does everyone have to know the Quality Policy verbatim without looking at all? Can they peek slightly?" I inquired.

"Well Mr. Sabuwala, if your staff does not know your quality policy, how will they share your vision? So yes, they should know it verbatim. But of course, no one can stop them from looking around. It's not a school exam," was Mr. Kulkarni's stern answer. He was a strict, disciplined man who always went by the rule book, but diplomatically suggested a solution to my query also.

"One more question, Mr. Kulkarni. It's regarding the files that the auditors choose for inspection. Will they pull out a file randomly, or can we suggest to them which file to inspect?" was my second question which further scorned Mr. Kulkarni's face.

"Mr. Sabuwala, you seem to be eager to figure out the loopholes in the audit. Simply speaking, the auditors can inspect files selected randomly, but they'll be courteous enough to not directly pick-up the files themselves. They will not ransack your office to search for hidden files. They'll ask you to give them a file for inspection. They'll not be very stringent,this being your first audit. Instead of checking for one hundred percent compliance, they will be more interested in knowing whether you have understood the system in depth and will be able to follow the system in future," was Mr. Kulkarni's sharp remark.

"Thanks Mr. Kulkarni, we'll be prepared for the audit and we'll try not to let you down," was my courteous reply.

****

Friday, 10th September 2010. Two days before the foundation anniversary of Dessign7 was our very first ISO audit. All procedure we had outlined and set for the organization, since the last three months, would be audited for perfection by an external auditor - a stranger who neither understood us nor our business. Our trainer since the last three months would not be present to assist us in our moment of truth. All of a sudden, our minds were highlighting the grey areas in the Quality Manual, not completely understood by us; we were unsure about our ability to confront the probing questions. "Pre-exam jitters," I recalled Mr. Kulkarni's assuring words, "Don't worry, you have worked hard and you are absolutely prepared for the audit."

We were prepared for the audit, but a little nervousness was inevitable. We checked the items on our list of things to do:-

We ensured that the staff had memorized the Quality Policy.

- ✓ We framed multiple copies of the Quality Policy such that at least one of them easily legible from anywhere in the office - a saving grace in case anyone forgot it.
- ✓ We imparted a crash course to the staff on the procedures outlined in the Quality Manual.
- ✓ We segregated the files which were to be given to the auditors for inspection.
- ✓ We confirmed from our site supervis or that all drawings and documents on site were updated, neatly filed and readily available for inspection.

The stage was set for a perfect audit

Incidentally, on that particular, important day, I had a few prospective clients (a term derived during the ISO training) from Italy wanting to explore the business opportunities in India. It was a three-day, pre-planned tripand we were scheduled to conduct a market survey for their products in Pune, Mumbai and Bengaluru. That particular day, I was to escort them around the city of Pune, thereby being unable to be present for the entire audit. Although I was aware of my appointment, I waited till the last moment to break the news to Anagha and Rachna. I knew they wouldn't approve of my absence from the audit and I didn't want to postpone the date of the audit. After a little persuasion, I managed to convince them to face the auditors without me. The baton was firmly held by the two ladies next-in-charge.

The entire office strictly was dressed in formal attire to welcome the auditors for an opening meeting at 10:00 am. Upon the request of the auditors, I was present for the opening meeting and had committed to be present for the closing meeting as well. After the opening meeting, Anagha and Rachna explained the work-flow process of the organization to the auditors. They reviewed the quality manual and asked for random samples of documents and records that were to be maintained as part of the new system. Rachna immediately handed them a file from the short listed pile of completed files. An in-depth scrutiny of files followed and the auditors recorded their observations to be discussed in the closing meeting. Rachna and Anagha confidently replied to every question hurled at them. Even I had my share of questions from the Italians, but they were more generic and, therefore, less taxing.

After lunch, a site visit was arranged for the auditors to check the implementation of procedure on site. This was Rachna's homeland for the battle. Rachna had meticulously planned for the site visit. She had specifically selected a site where the work was at an initial stages. Considering that there wasn't much development on that site, the auditors couldn't ask too many questions.

"What is the scope of work defined for execution here?" an auditor asked.

"We have undertaken a design and build contract for the entire house. Right now the tiling work is in progress." Rachna answered.

"What precautions will you take while laying the existing tiles,to prevent water seepage into the floor below?"

"There is not much that can be done to prevent the seepage. However, with the client's consent, we requested co-operation from their neighbour below,in turn promising them to re-paint their ceiling and walls if they got damaged due to the seepage," Rachna replied.

"Is the cost of re-painting the neighbors flat considered in your estimate? Why can't you waterproof the slab?"

"We can't waterproof the slab because it is not designed to take additional waterproofing load. Also, theoretically speaking, it will be more economical to do a coat of paint for the neighbor than to entirely waterproof this apartment. And yes! The client has approved the cost of painting the neighbor's apartment, if necessary." Rachna paused, indicating that she was ready for the next question.

"What about safety measures for workers on site?" another auditor asked.

"We are not in a heavy construction industry where laborers are required to wear helmets, rubber boots or any other safety gear. However, we always maintain a first-aid kit on site for minor injuries that can occur," Rachna said, pointing to the white box hung on the wall.

"But I see a lot of wires hanging from the ceiling and walls. What if someone gets an electric shock? You should have at least sealed the wires with an insulation tape."

"The wires are not live. They were disconnected from the main board before we started any work on site. It is our regular practice in order to prevent any accidents. The workers are provided with temporary electric boards for running their equipment." Rachna replied, confidently holding a loose wire.

There was no way that the non-technical auditors would get the better of her on site queries. The files were well updated on site, the laborers were trained to speak only when spoken to, and Rachna's knowledge was unmatched. This session she won hands down.

I rejoined the auditors and my colleagues for the closing meeting where a few minor queries were raised and two minor non-conformities were identified. With promises of getting them rectified before the next internal audit, we were awarded the ISO certification. Dessign7 was now ISO certified. Our heads were high with pride as we entered the league of firms with the coveted status.

Lots of stories of the day's happenings were exchanged amongst us, highlighting the strong and weak moments of the day. Excitement filled us and our reactions could not be expressed in words. It was only the next day that I rewarded the ladies with an appreciation note and a bouquet for their diligent effort.

Anagha and Rachna were achievers of the year.

Dessign7 had evolved to a higher status.

No one was asked to recite the Quality Policy.

***

Being ISO certified was a monumental achievement for us, and if this was a movie, I am sure we would have celebrated with dinner, drinks and dance; but in reality, life had just become more hectic. If we expected clients to follow our processes, we had to first become flawless. But once we got used to it, QMS seemed invaluable.

QMS enlightened us about two important aspects of business growth. Firstly, it was necessary to standardize drawings and procedures wherever possible; and secondly, how to systematically file drawings and documents for easy future reference. We developed rigid documentations and recorded every decision and approval given by a client. We also set stages of design approval without which we would not proceed to the next level of designing; and after the approval, we would deter clients from going back to revisit the decision. "There are a million design combinations possible with your place at this stage and what we need to do is peg down things one at time. Sometimes, curbs are required to define the road; otherwise one can stray into the jungles," Rachna often told a client hesitating to sign in the approval column.

"Interior designing is a creative field, but we at Dessign7 believe that designers are not pure artists. We are technocrats. We carefully study the function of a space before we start designing it. We optimize the utility of the space and sensitively blend the utilitarian components with the appropriate artistic appeal to create a complete design experience." -This was our design philosophy.

We split our design process into two stages – the utility stage and the aesthetic stage. We gave more importance to designing the utility of a place because if a place wasn't optimally utilized, we considered it as a design failure. Designing the utility was governed by standard anthropometric data and a wrong design could be objectively proved. Aesthetic designing was, however, subjective. We realized that although the aesthetic want of a client can vary drastically depending on an individual's choice, the utility of a place is more or less standard with fewer possible permutations and combinations. Therefore, we focused on standardization of utility drawings. Rachna started the mammoth task of creating a library of utility drawings which would be a ready reference for every client. She assigned her dedicated juniors to search,collect and compile our scattered treasures to create a design catalogue.

Days were spent scanning the complete data of old drawings. In-depth scrutiny of drawing files was done and the useful data was assembled into a common folder.

Categories of drawings were mutually discussed and defined to make accessibility of relevant drawings easier. The sub-classification had to be rigid enough to stand the test of time, yet flexible enough to accommodate any afterthoughts. Once the drawings were assigned to their new sub-folders, we had to work on their presentation. Each and every drawing had to have the same format, so that it was a branded product of Dessign7. Its unique identity was important to convey the professionalism of Dessign7. Rachna designed and implemented the format for the catalogue. It took nearly three months of work before our first design catalogue was ready. And years later, we continue to add more designs every month to each section of the catalogue.

Rachna's effort in creating the design catalogue paid up well. New clients browsed through a ready catalogue of standard designs and short listed the designs they liked. The non-experimental clients with limited visualization, asked us to replicate one of the short listed designs depending on what we felt would be appropriate for their space. The others - more adventurous clients - asked us to customize the designs, incorporating some design elements they had seen elsewhere or imagined at some time. In both the cases, for us it served dual purpose. Firstly, it helped us to gauge the client's expectation of his project;secondly, it created a well-informed platform for our further discussions with him. Also, customizing a short listed design is much easier than creating a new design from scratch. There are times when innovative concepts had faced the client's rejection due to lack of visualization on his part, resulting in a loss of mutual effort and time,in an era where everyone wanted everything at internet speed. Instead of innovating for all clients, we preferred to customize a short listed design as per the client's requirements and tastes. This gave him a clear visualization of the design and also expedited the design processes. But most importantly it formed the basis of a future business model – the franchising of Dessign7.

Growing Business

9

On a casual Sunday morning, just after the October monsoons, I happened to visit an exhibition boasting of new business opportunities, which gave business ideas on a platter! Pleased that the new systems were being implemented in office effectively, courtesy the joint efforts of Rachna and Anagha, I decided to explore this window of opportunity. Normally, my Sundays are allergic to work but then this wasn't work exactly, so I strolled into the exhibition for a meager entrance fee.

It was an exhibition with approximately sixty stalls of various sizes,proportionate to the size of a company and its brand value. I walked around the crowded aisles, browsing through the stalls and quickly grasped a gist of the variety of business opportunities the exhibitors were offering. In the second round, I interacted with business companies from various sectors to understand their business models. I would broadly categorize the business into two types - the product-based model and the concept-based model.

In the product-based segment, I encountered designer garment manufacturers, who wanted prospective retail store owners to display and sell their products. Then there were arrange of coffee shop franchisors, who were ready to woo the crowd with addictive coffees;after all it was the fastest growing business in Pune, considering that 'a lot could happen over coffee'. Coffee shops were the right places for activities ranging from business deals to dates. The ever indulging youngsters were always ready to explore a new joint. Hence,a coffee shop franchise was a hot proposition for most people looking for a new business avenue. I even came across a few restaurant owners wanting to add new outlets through the medium of franchising.

Concept-based franchisors majorly included various play schools and real estate broking firms. In this segment, play schools or educational institutes offering various kinds of personality grooming courses were the most popular. Eager parents wanting to give their kids a competitive edge are willing to do anything - right from early schooling to personality grooming. In India, educationalists are placed on high pedestals, and therefore, an educational institute was the most sought after franchise in the concept segment.

After detailed interactions with franchisors from various segments and collecting a bagful of brochures, I headed home lamenting about half a precious Sunday lost without lazing, but proud about the day being very educative.

The next few days kept us busy with site hand overs for people wanting to move into their new abodes during the auspicious days of Diwali. We were ourselves very keen to finish the projects due for handover, knowing well that the upcoming holiday season would see a lot of labor shortage. Also not wanting work to spill over into our coveted week-long Diwali break was motivation enough to work tirelessly.

Rachna spent her holiday with family, engrossed in celebrating the most important festival of India. It's customary for friends and relatives to visit each other's houses to exchange greetings for the season. Our visit to Rachna's house was on the second day of Diwali. We had carried a special gift for her, something she coveted for a long time and I was eager to see her reaction.

When we entered Rachna's place, Palak and Devika's were already waiting there. "Hi! What a coincidence? When did you guys come?" Anagha inquired.

"Hi! We have been here since sometime. And we were about to leave, but Rachna informed us that you were on your way, so we stayed to meet up with all of you," Devika said.

"So what are you guys up to? Where are you working now?" I asked looking at Palak.

"I have joined Bookworm.com and I write online articles on various topics," Palak informed me about her shift in the career.

"Good, an absolute shift in the career and a desk job like the one you always wanted," I replied.

"Yes, definitely! No hassles dealing with contractors and no ill-timed panic calls from clients," Palak said flashing a broad smile.

"True, but I am sure no fancy Diwali gifts also from your bosses," I said sarcastically, waving the wrapped gift we were carrying for Rachna. I was looking at the streak of jealousy on Palak's face. Her broad smile had narrowed. Then I enquired turning to Devika, "And how's your practice going?"

"We are doing quite well," Devika responded in the same soft-spoken voice, "We get a few leads from Pestonjee Builders and references from friends too. And how has work been for you, sir?"

"Great! Rachna's managing all the designing and site work. I concentrate more on marketing and sales now. We recently implemented ISO systems. Huge change in our working style. Can you imagine an organized and disciplined office of a designer?"

"Yeah, all the time that we spent playing games is now utilized to keep client files updated." Rachna remarked.

"Nowadays we play a new game. Spot the error in filing order," Anagha said.

"And once you spot your first error, you have to shout UNO," Shirin joked. We all laughed.

"But seriously, quite a lot of improvements since you guys left and we are enjoying the discipline," I said glancing towards Rachna and she was grinning amused at the last teasing statement.

The casual conversation continued as we munched on the savories and sweets. Customary to Diwali, Anagha gave Rachna her gift. She must have received lots of gifts from friends and family, but her excitement was expressed with a thrilling shriek when she opened the wrapping to find something she much desired – the iPhone 4. She had tears in eyes as she jumped with joy, thanking us for the gift.

She spent the next few days flaunting the Apple product to friends explaining the perks of working with Dessign7. It's amazing how a much-coveted object becomes even more precious when it's a gift from people you love and respect. As for us, we wanted to appreciate Rachnaforher dedication and effort for becoming such a strong pillar of support; the iPhone was just a medium.

Anagha and I had a relaxed Diwali break. Anagha utilized the mornings to escort Shirin to her friends' houses to distribute chocolates especially prepared for them, whilst we met up with friends and family in the evenings. Any spare time was utilized well by watching blockbusters released during Diwali.

I was deeply engrossed for the first three days working on a one thousand-piece puzzle, which is a Diwali holiday ritual for me. But the next four days, I spent studying the franchise brochures I had previously collected. I meticulously studied every brochure to understand its business offering. I analyzed each and every business model forits core product or concept that it offered to a prospective franchisee. I made mental notes of the salient features of every business and on the brochure itself, I highlighted with a marker, the key aspects of every offer. I even studied the graphical representation of information in the brochure and arrived at the optimum content that any franchise brochure has to have to sell its concept to a prospective franchisee. I spotted and identified the common threads in all brochures, which formed the basic framework of every franchising business. I jotted down a list of important information that any franchisor needs to convey to a prospective franchisee:-

- ✓ Growth of the industry in the current market
- ✓ Information about the franchisor's company and its experience
- ✓ Franchise fees and tenure of agreement
- ✓ Projected growth of a franchisee
- ✓ Breakeven time for the franchisee for the franchise fees
- ✓ Frequently asked questions

The opportunities, the promises, the base products and basic business proposals were common. They all offered only one thing to the franchisee - their experience. In the next couple of days,I built a new business framework using this knowledge.

Interior designing is a growing industry in India, owing to the belief that a good, self-owned home is a highly-valued achievement of one's life. Also, in a country where labor is abundantly available, even an averaged-income person prefers to get his house professionally refurbished by an experienced and well-known agency. The do-it-yourself culture has still not crept in. Dessign7 had sufficient experience and expertise in the field of interior designing. It had a vast portfolio of clients in both, residential and commercial sectors. With the Quality Management System successfully implemented, it was one of the most organized agencies in the industry. Also, we had created an exhaustive catalogue of designs which would help our associates to simplify their design process. I thought and rethought the business concept and began to elaborate upon the vague outline I had initially created. Ireturned to the office from the vacation with a fresh new business idea.

As I entered office, I handed over my bag of franchise brochures to Manzoor, our marketing executive, to study them in depth. Towards noon, when everyone in the office was well settled and Rachna had assigned the day's work to the juniors, I invited her, Anagha and Manzoor for a management meeting. I announced to all with a huge smile,

"Dessign7 will expand. The franchising way."

***

"Dessign7 is going to grow further through franchising," as I spoke, I could see blank faces staring at me. I had achieved the desired effect; now it was time for me to explain my statement. "Go through these brochures," I said as I took the brochures from Manzoor and placed the brochures on the table in front of everyone for them to start browsing. "These entrepreneurs have expanded their business through franchising. If you notice, there are two types of franchisors, either selling a product or selling a concept. But, actually what they are all really selling is their experience. Franchisors selling products also sell soft skills training, client retention techniques, product innovation, pricing, etc. to a franchisee along with just various coffee mixes. Training institutes on the other hand have tried to make their teachings tangible by devising strict course material. A real estate broking firm is cashing in by selling a whole network of other brokers registered as its franchisee. Also it is selling virtual presence on its well-branded and advertised website. So, in short, they are all selling experience and they are imparting this experience through training," I continued as I handed over the short listed, well-designed brochures to everyone to study. As they were studying the highlighted points in every brochure, I continued, "For the last four days, I have thought about the positives of these models and I am very optimistic, so I want to hear about any drawbacks or negatives that you can think of," and I rested my case to the small jury for a verdict. There was a brief pause before all of us indulged in a long session, discussing the pros and cons with a unanimous conclusion. We were going to create our franchise model.

Over the next few days, we enlisted all the items of work to be done before we could launch our franchise business and distributed responsibilities amongst ourselves, depending upon our respective job profiles. The most important task, necessary for this venture, was to upgrade the company credentials and its brand value. Dessign7 was a proprietary firm, without its own independent identity. It would portray an impression of a small firm and this would not give the requisite confidence to a prospective franchisee to associate with us. After consulting our chartered accountants, "Dessign7" was re-christened "Dessign7 Interiors Pvt. Ltd",by converting it from a proprietary firm to a private limited company. We registered this name immediately and it was used on all future official documentation. The company's new name and its independent legal status enhanced the organization image. The next logical step was to enhance our virtual image.

I believed in the philosophy that "you never get a second chance to create a first impression," and in the age of technology, the company's first impression is usually created by its website. Any prospective franchisee would definitely visit our website before he would approach us for further discussion. Hence, our website needed a new look, having an international appeal, in synch with the company image we desired for our new venture.

M/s. Webmasters was a client of ours with expertise in creating websites for clients in the UK and the USA. We entrusted our website development to their expertise. We studied websites of various international design houses and finalized an appropriate look to reflect our image. As compared to our previous website, we decided to make the new website content based and well optimized for the Google search engines. Rachna researched, collected and created technical content, offering free design tips to a casual guest visiting the website, whereas a serious client could gauge our ability through the actual site photographs displayed in our design gallery. Anagha and I worked on the minor finishing of the website to ensure it had a crisp look. We also dedicated a prime position on the top right hand side corner of the home page for giving additional mileage to our franchisees. A section enlisting the franchisees was also incorporated in the website. The new power-packed website was uploaded and live.

A new, crisp and dynamic image of the company was created, but it had to be marketed well to make it a popular brand. We set aside a hefty advertising budget to promote the brand of Dessign7 Interiors Pvt. Ltd through various print media, radio ads and even television. We were funding the entire campaign with our own savings and therefore, the resources were very dear. I critically analyzed every marketing proposal, evaluated the reach of the media and the audience it targeted. Negotiation was my forte and I drove a hard bargain to get the best deals. Anagha helped me to plan and space out the campaigns, so that we could track its effectiveness. We successfully kick started our brand-building activities.

Manzoor was given the responsibility of creating a list of new geographies we could expand to. He researched online and made a list of all the cities - within a range of three hundred kilometers from Pune – where we could launch the first phase of our franchise program. Manzoor prepared a data sheet of the cities, their population, prospective growth of the city, major industries in the zone and its accessibility from Pune. Manzoor also identified and spoke to interior designing colleges where we could conduct a seminar on our franchising program for fresh graduates. I considered it as a viable medium to educate young entrepreneurs on how to partner with us to soar high faster.

Rachna updated the design catalogue constantly. New concepts and designs were continuously added to enrich the design catalogue. This library would be an important bonus that a franchisee would receive from us. Rachna also created the content for the website and the franchise brochure.

Like I mentioned earlier, everyone was focused on

completing their respective tasks, working towards our company's vision. Our vision was crystal clear - to make Dessign7 Interiors Pvt. Ltd a nationally preferred brand for interior designing.

Amongst the development of all the marketing collaterals for franchising and building of the Dessign7 brand, what remained top priority of our franchise program was the experience sharing through training. It was Rachna's and my responsibility to develop a detailed training program for a new franchisee. The training program was designed to cover all aspects of the interior designing business, from marketing one's services to a new client, to handover of the completed site to him. It was an exhaustive task, but training a franchisee to understand your business model, adopt it and follow it thoroughly was the key to mutual success. It was the creation of our own training program that saw the next leap of evolution in Rachna's career.

And it also brought back a friend from the past.

The Past Returns 10

Palak Lalwani had left Dessign7 because she was bored of interior designing and she desired a change in career. And true to her word, she never looked back upon interior designing and had chosen to forget about it, until we decided to awaken the past. She was working as a content writer or a cyber-journalist for a USA-based multi-national company called Bookworm.com. She wrote articles on various topics which were published online. She was also freelancing as a content writer for a few website developers and had completed a couple of assignments as a ghost writer. Well aware of Palak's writing career, Rachna suggested that she could be considered as a good option to help us pen down our training program. But first we had to prepare a detailed framework of the training program ourselves.

Being a techno-commercial training program, Rachna and I had accepted the responsibility of authoring the same. First, we developed the skeleton of the training program based on the company process flowchart. We readily referred to our Quality Manual for the same. After we enlisted all the topics, we realized that the Quality

Manual only covered the technical aspect of the business. A complete training program has to not only provide the technical knowledge – which is usually available in colleges – but also be augmented with soft skills training that a start-up entrepreneur would require.

We started preparing our training program with an exhaustive module on marketing strategies and sales etiquette. Over time, I had gained sufficient knowledge of various marketing media available and the effectiveness of every medium relevant to the field of interior designing. We covered cost-effective ways of marketing one's services and scripted a perfect sales pitch that would ensure a definite client closure. We spelled out those ten critical questions, which if answered well can win a client's confidence. Obviously knowing the right answers was our first key to success, and that's where our expertise would benefit a franchisee.

The second key to success was our competitive pricing. Good negotiation skills plays an important part in offering a competitive pricing to clients, but these skills are never taught in designing colleges. Negotiation is not about getting the cheapest price for a product. It involves a careful evaluation of various proposals you receive for a particular product or service and then arriving at the most optimum cost for it. You might not always give the contract to the lowest bidder, but you still have to justify your decision. My philosophy always said that "you never leave a negotiation table till the deal is sealed". These chapters covered purely the commercial aspects of the business. The core technical aspects of the business were covered in the next few chapters.

Rachna and I wanted our entire design process to be covered in the training program with utmost detail. We visualized the entire designing process and dissected it into smaller processes. We penned down all aspects of the business starting from conducting a site survey to creating conceptual drawing and completing the design process with detailed working drawings. Rachna took the lead in framing the content for the designing and site execution module. She included even basic topics like taking site photographs during a site survey or getting a contractor to mark the design on site, before executing it. She authored a detailed section on site execution, listing various stages, highlighting critical check points, detailed inspection of completed work to a hassle free handover Rachna handled the technical section of the training program very well.

Although Rachna could independently handle the technical part of the training program, our joint effort was required to frame the techno-commercial modules. It was this part of the module which would form the crux of our training. Any young entrepreneur who would become our franchisee would probably be confident of creating a design, but the true art lies in convincing the client to accept the design. The use of right vocabulary and floral language is very necessary. A designer should have the ability to create a visual walk-through for the client by using his words only. Another problem that young entrepreneurs face is that they can't explain a site execution error or site handover delay to the client, without souring their relationship with them. Our training program included answers to such problems and effective tips for interacting with the client.

Our final module included chapters on effective techniques to amicably settle all site related issues with clients; bask in the glory during a house warming function and methods on networking with the existing clients to effectively get more references of new clients.

Once the program outline was ready, we needed an expert to write down our thoughts, because none of us was a writer in the first place. Since Rachna had suggested Palak's name as a writer, and I didn't know any other ghost writer, I asked Rachna to immediately contact the only writing expert we knew.

It had been few years since Palak had come to our office for an official reason. Although, all of us had been in touch over many social occasions, we had never interacted for official work. Palak reached the office by 7:00 pm sharp, immediately after her office hours. As she was entering the office, she glanced on the left side of the door, noticing the absence of pizza boxes which had once lured her to join Dessign7 as trainee. Rachna and Palak entered the cabin, made themselves comfortable in the chairs in front of me and all of us started a casual conversation. Palak informed us more about her job at Bookworm.com, her ambition to start a wedding magazine – to which I agreed to fund the project if she wanted a financial partner – and about some of her freelancing works. I explained to her about the progress of Dessign7 Interior Pvt Ltd, showed her photographs of some of our recent projects and told her about our ambitious franchise program. Rachna continued the discussion further, "So, basically for training the franchisees, we need to devise a training program. We have already prepared and well-defined the outline of the program and we even have pointers for each topic, but we needed someone to pen down our thoughts and frame it in proper grammatical sentences."

"So, basically you require a ghost writer?" Palak flaunted her technical language.

"Yes! And when we thought of a ghost, we thought of you!" I quipped, "I mean we don't know anyone scarier!"

"Oh please sir!" Palak brushed the comment with a grin.

Rachna completely ignored my comment, she asked Palak, "So will you be able to take it up?"

"Sure I'll be able to take it up. What is the approximate quantum of the document? Let me know and I'll revert with a time frame and a lump sum cost for the entire work."

"Palak, you'll charge us for it?" I asked humorously, "I mean, after all these years that we have trained and tolerated you in Dessign7, you are asking for money?!?"

"Oh please sir!" Palak repeated and I thought to myself that for a writer, she surely didn't use a wide variety of vocabulary.

"On a serious note, don't give a lump sum quote. We'll pay you as per the word count, as we are not sure on how extensive the document will be and I don't want you to feel overburdened once you have quoted a figure." I said earnestly.

"Palak, how do we go about the entire project? How do we convey the matter to you?" Rachna asked, realizing the practical problem on hand. As Palak had a full time job, she'd only find time to work on the project in the evenings.

"That's pretty simple! Record your thoughts on a recorder, one section at a time. Once you are done with each section, send me the audio file. I'll listen to the file, pen your thoughts onto paper, rephrase it to ensure proper flow of content and resend the written document to you for approval," Palak seemed crystal clear about the entire process, which reflected her confidence and assured me that she was the right choice for the assignment.

"Palak, that sounds perfect. Send me a quote and we'll freeze it tomorrow itself. Also, we'll keep the first chapter ready for you by tomorrow evening. That sounds good?" I asked, eager for her to start working on the training program. I assumed her answer to be positive, so before she could reply, I shot out another question, "So when and where is the treat for bagging the new project? Rachna, is there any new, expensive Chinese restaurants in town?" All of us had a hearty laugh, recalling Palak's first treat in Dessign7.

The next day, I approved Palak's quote, without negotiating too much and she started with her work on the training program. She and Rachna followed the system with clockwork precision. Every evening, once we were done with the day's work, we recorded our expertise and experience in words on every aspect of the business, tackling one section at a time. We mailed the audio recording to Palak, who penned it down as a text file and sent the initial draft to us, by the following morning. Throughout the next day, we proofread the draft, made necessary alterations and sent it back to her for final checking and finishing. She checked the final draft added the appropriate punctuation marks to improve the legibility of the document; rectified any grammatical errors and provided suitable titles to every section. Simultaneously, new set of recordings for the next section was sent, and the same process was repeated. This exchange of information, facilitated by advanced means of electronic data storage and communication, worked perfectly well. Rachna and I were excited with the way the training program was shaping up. Palak had excelled in the assignment, and for once, I was glad that she chose writing over interior designing. She did very well.

For Rachna and myself, preparing the "Training Manual", as we now called it, was opening a whole new world of experience. Neither Rachna, nor I had ever done anything like this before. As we started authoring each section, we realized that a human mind can store so much of information, which we so casually use in our daily lives, without realizing that this information can be invaluable and precious to an inexperienced person. Our entire thought process, which governs our success in life, is truly valuable business acumen. When this business acumen is well documented, it becomes a powerful training program which forms the basis of any franchise business model.

Towards the completion of the "Training Manual" we added a few pages on the importance and usage of every document that was a part of the client file. We knew that if a franchisee knew the importance of every document he was expected to use, then he would be more inclined to truly follow it rather than dismiss it as unnecessary paperwork. Palak completed the 'Training Manual' by adding a foreword, table of contents and a paragraph about the authors. We ended up with a two hundred and fifty page document with a collective business experience of fifteen years and, therefore, christened it "15 years in a Nutshell". Alas, our business and our expertise, derived out of our experience, were now documented and readily available for training a novice who has just entered the business. Our final step to launching our franchise program was complete. We were now ready to invite prospective franchisees.

And it also brought back a ghost from the past.

***

"But we will have to find some way to reduce the cost, this is way above our budget," spoke Sneha with a drooping face, constantly complaining to Rachna since the last thirty minutes. Sneha's expressions were personified emoticons that one would attach with a text message. She stole a glance at Anand- her husband- with an exaggerated droop, to gauge his reaction to the entire estimate just presented to them. Anand and Sneha had appointed us to design their recently purchased dream home – a four-bedroom bungalow in the outskirts of the city. Sneha, being from a family of businessmen, was a seasoned negotiator whose expertise lied in getting a little more for every rupee spent. She attempted the question one more time hoping for a favorable answer.

"How can we reduce the cost?"

"Well, if we want to reduce the cost," explained Rachna, "the only way would be to either reduce the quality of the material or to reduce the quantity of the work. I don't think we want to compromise on the quality; after all we want it to last for a minimum of fifteen years, right?" Mr. and Mrs. Oberoi nodded in agreement.

"Then the next way would be to reduce the quantity of work," Rachna paused. She gauged the effect of her words and then continued, "Let's see, from the estimate, if we reduce the size of wardrobe in the master bedroom to say two-thirds, then the total square feet quantity of wardrobe will come down substantially. We'll get a huge saving. There," Rachna proved her point by making a few quick changes on the spreadsheet displayed on the monitor and reduced the total of the estimate.

"No Anand, we'll require the wardrobe in the master bedroom. We can't reduce that," sulked Sneha to Anand, who was by now convinced that the conversation was going nowhere. Rachna had played her cards well. She knew no client would accept the words 'compromise in quality' for their dream home; and Sneha would never agree to reduce her wardrobe space. So the original estimate was approved in its entirety. But, Rachna offered them a perk. She had to ensure that they didn't leave the negotiation without feeling that they didn't benefit out of it. Rachna finally offered a one percent, pre-decided discount but made them feel that they earned it. Vaishali, who was assisting Rachna in the meeting, noted how her mentor tackled the client and only smiled in admiration.

The evolution cycle was now complete. The evolution of this butterfly was now complete and was ready to soar high. Rachna's understanding of the business was achieving perfection with every passing day. Her client relations and negotiation skills were constantly improving. She was independently managing designers; getting stage-wise approvals from the clients in accordance with the QMS; coordinating with vendors and contractors; attending and solving any crisis on sites and even following up with clients for payments. Anagha handled the administration, finances and HR perfectly. Thus, my focus had graduated from designing and site execution to brand building, marketing and improving sales.

With our new marketing strategies and brand-building activities, we received a lot of inquiries for our services. The calls had to be responded to professionally and constant follow-up was required with prospective clients until they either finally awarded the project to us or confirmed that they had given the project to another designer. Zeenat was the ideal candidate for this profile.

Zeenat was our oldest employee amongst the current staff, Rachna being second in line. Zeenat came from a moderate class family and was a single parent to her daughter Zainab, who was studying in a college in Mumbai. Zeenat was staying with her parents, partially supporting the household income with her salary. She had joined Dessign7 as a receptionist, but her profile was eventually extended to administrative work; now I wanted her to venture into sales. Although Zeenat was not a very convincing salesperson, she had certain advantages which made her a suitable candidate for the job. Being with us for over six years now, she understood the business activities of Dessign7 sufficiently well to explain them to any inquiring client. She was well-versed in English, Hindi and Marathi - the three languages necessary to converse fluently with any client. Also, she needed the extra incentive offered to her for every client she converted; hence, she would give every client her best shot. Lastly, her current profile left her with sufficient time in hand to take up the additional responsibility.

Rachna and I had already covered procedure for telephone marketing extensively in our training manual, "15 years in a Nutshell". We had detailed out the entire script, which one could use to introduce our company to a prospective client, over the phone. We had also listed down some common questions frequently asked by clients and the corresponding, ideal answers to these questions. This section was given to Zeenat, as a ready reference, for study and practice. Once she was confident enough to deliver the script, she gave mock calls to us. With our constant inputs, she soon attained a fairly good flow of Dessign7's introductory speech. It was now Zeenat's job to filter incoming inquiry calls and set up an appointment for Rachna, Anagha or me, depending upon our availability. Maximum calls were diverted to me and incase I was not available the meetings were conducted by Anagha or Rachna. Zeenat seemed like a good prospective marketing pillar for Dessign7 Interiors Pvt. Ltd.

The system was dynamic and all of us enjoyed the momentum of work. Anagha and I enjoyed building the organization; Rachna enjoyed her authority in the firm and Zeenat enjoyed the additional income. We were ambitious about the new organizational structure, but yet again, I neglected that ambition can undermine the foundation of any pillar.

***

When we finally launched our franchise model, we first decided to offer the proposal to the ex-staff who had at different stages contributed to the growth of Dessign7 Interiors Pvt. Ltd. We made a list of this extended family and evidently the first name that came to my mind was Rajesh Chaudhary.

Rajesh was sacked from Dessign7 for inappropriate conduct, but I always had a soft corner for him and he had shown enough respect over the last three years by constantly wishing me, without fail, on my birthday and of course, Teacher's Day. Time always changes people for the better. Although Anagha and I parented Dessign7, Rajesh had been the godfather of this young child at its nascent stage and when an opportunity came to reconnect them both, I forgave and forgot.

Proposals and brochures were couriered to all the ex-employees and as expected, Rajesh was the first to respond. We set up an appointment immediately and I explained the entire business model to him. I also briefed him on his responsibility as franchisee and our role as a franchisor. Lastly, I informed him of the franchise fee that he would be required to pay and additionally, to encourage him to be the premier franchisee, I offered him a discount on it. I could read the enthusiasm in his eyes as he attentively heard the entire proposal. Also, he appreciated the rebate offered to him. Once I completed my explanation, he spoke in improved but still distorted English, "Good progresssir! I hear a lot of Dessign7 ads on radio and seen ads in some magazines also. Dessign7 is becoming well-known brand in interiors. And your franchise scheme is super-duper. Good scheme sir; I like a lot and want to join, but at the time I don't have full payment. Can I pay some part now and rest later in timely installment? I really want to become part of you people." Rajesh was just the same - bold, confident and still lacking finesse. Rajesh had a small setup by now to execute turnkey interior projects, but yet couldn't be the face of his own firm, owing to his unrefined stance. He took assistance from AaronJames, an interior designer who was employed with Hallmark Cards, coordinating with us as the company's representative, when we were executing Hallmark Card Stores all across India. Aaron was an average designer with limited exposure to the interior designing industry. He was only suitable for designing small budget projects. Rajesh understood that his growth with Aaron would always be limited, and if he was supported by the brand name and profile of Dessign7, he could pitch for much larger projects. On the other hand, I had an affinity for Rajesh, having trained him for so many years, and wanted him to ally with us. I believed that an improved and loyal Rajesh would be an asset to the company, so I flexed the payment options for him. We agreed to register the agreement on the first available auspicious date and we shook hands as he left my cabin.

"Hi Zeenat, long time we not met. How are you? How is work? What are you doing now?" questioned Rajesh as he met Zeenat sitting at the reception desk with a phone in her hand.

"I have graduated from receptionist to marketing. I handle client inquiries on phone," she replied, proud of her progress in the firm. "What brings you here today, after such a long time?"

"Sir called, I am taking Dessign7 franchise, we already agree to sign up," came the answer and as Rajesh made his way into the studio, he spotted Rachna, who was occupying his previous cubicle.

"Hi Rachna, so now you occupy my seat. Too much you progress here," he spoke in a bitter tone, "But all headache also yours. You manage well or need my help? Some tips I can give if you want," he added to cover his bitterness with sarcastic humor.

"Ah Rajesh! Actually I enjoy this position a lot. And if I take your tips, I'll be out of the company itself," Rachna returned the sarcasm. "We have ironed out the previous execution flaws with our new working systems. We manage projects a lot more smoothly, unlike before. Previously, in sir's absence, there wasn't a competent guide for the juniors, but now I guide my juniors well. So now our sites are completed more efficiently."

"Sir offered me franchise and I'll soon be part of Dessign7, working together with you, again!" Rajesh spoke, hoping to instill his fear in Rachna. "It will be fun!"

"You bet it'll be fun, though I am not sure how much you'll enjoy it. By the way, I suggested to sir that the first franchise be offered to you. I thought it'll be fun working with you, and besides it would give you a chance to progress with Dessign7. AGAIN!"

"No not like that! My business grow a lot. I have my own office and my own identity. I have established myself, not still stuck in same office after so many years. Here my card," Rajesh spoke proudly as he handed his business card to Rachna.

"Rajesh, having a business card does not mean that you have a business! After so many years you are here, back in Dessign7, lamenting the loss of your position. Growing independently is a challenge. Ally with us and your growth will be unlimited. And don't worry, I promise you that it'll be fun!" Rachna retorted.

The bold and confident Rajesh was speechless. He extended a hand to wish goodbye and with a slight hesitation Rachna returned the gesture. The face-off was evident as determined looks were exchanged. Their boldness and confidence was on par. Rachna, secure in her position, returned to her work on the computer and Rajesh gave a coveted look to his cubicle as he turned around to leave the office.

11 The Face Off

The first phase of franchise marketing went quite well. We had already signed up Rajesh as the first franchisee and we received a mix bag of responses from the other ex-employees. Palak, obviously had given up on interiors so she expressed regret. Aaisha was pursuing postgraduate studies in project management. Devika and Shahnawaz had a stable practice of their own and although we met them on various occasions thereafter, none of us broached the topic. A few boys had moved out of Pune to continue with their family business and a couple of girls were not too keen on pursuing a career after their marriage. We also had two positive responses. The first positive response was from Rahul, our electrical contractor. He had experience in contracting and the ability to read drawings, but lacked marketing skills for which he partnered with his well-spoken and well-networked friend, Nilesh. The second positive response was from Krishna, who was a part of Dessign7 and had left almost six months before Rachna joined. We did the pilot run of the franchise program in the control area of our city, with the three franchisees we had signed up.

The first assignment that we did with Rajesh was an office fit-out for M/s. Zenny Industries Ltd. As per QMS, we gave Rajesh the complete set of drawings - with client's approval on them, scope of work and timelines on the day we assigned the contract to him. Rajesh was surprised to see the evolution in Dessign7's working style. He was used to working with a system where drawings were prepared as the site progressed. Rachna explained the entire set to Rajesh. He heard the entire explanation and, with lots of effort found a few technical queries on which he had his own suggestions. Rachna downright discarded his suggestions and explained to him that working systems were now different. "Rajesh, we now use superior quality plywood, cut in required sections, to create the framework of partitions, instead of salwood, which we previously used. Although it's cheaper to use salwood, it usually develops cracks along the grains later on and that can compromise the strength of the partitions, hence we have stopped using it," Rachna explained the technical difference to him.

"But material cost, time to do job and labor cost go much higher. We previously also use salwood and it still lasted till now. I'll give you end result finish whatever you want but let me do my way, I got more experience than you," Rajesh retorted aggressively. Their discussion eventually led to an argument – a battle to prove who was more technically sound. It finally ended on a loud note, with Rachna firmly putting her foot down and exclaiming, "Rajesh, I appreciate your suggestions but this has to be done my way."

"I am fine, I don't mind doing your way but then I don't take responsibility of it!" Rajesh responded.

"If you can't take responsibility for the work done by you then leave the job. I'll find an alternate agency to do the job!"

I overheard tempers fly and invited Rajesh into the cabin for a discussion. I explained to him calmly but assertively, "Rachna is the design and technical head. She has the final verdict in all design related matters and even I don't interfere in them. If you keep having clashes with her, it'll become difficult for you to work with us. Don't let ego get in your way." Rajesh understood me very well. I had preached to him many a time before to curb his ego when it boiled down to client satisfaction and my preaching was often practiced by him diligently. As he was leaving the cabin, I made a final remark, "If you had shown a little more patience, you would be in her position today." He looked at me and shut the door behind him. He accepted Rachna's technical demand and executed the site as per it as it didn't affect him financially. But at Mrs. Deol's site, the dispute was financial.

Mrs. Deol's project was a luxurious residential bungalow located in the prestigious and prime suburbs of Pune, for which we had bagged the entire fit-out on a design and build contract. Supporting the new alliances formed through franchising, we sub-contracted the site execution to Rajesh. As per usual practice, a copy of the entire approved design set was handed over to Rajesh at the commencement of the site execution, with an in-depth design explanation briefed by Rachna. She even supervised the design marking on the site personally to ensure any miscommunication was avoided. Rajesh commenced the work promptly, after the mobilization advance was given to him.

A fortnight later, when Rajesh demanded a second payment, I instructed Rachna to check the progress of the site and advice whether a second payment could be released or not. She set up an appointment with Rajesh and punctually reached the site. She methodically verified the drawings with the work done on site and as she progressed from room to room her heart sank upon witnessing the fiasco that had been implemented there. "Rajesh, the quality of workmanship is just not up to the standards of Dessign7. Proper levels are not followed, the edges are not finished well and I am not happy with the joinery. I will not accept this and sir will scream his head out if he sees this. You will have to rectify whatever is possible but for most cases you'll have to redo the work at your own expense." Rachna brought to his notice an array of flaws which could have been acceptable in the company's initial years; but with time, experience and better paying clientele, we strived to achieve flawless workmanship. Our philosophy had graduated to 'Strive for perfection initially than rectify flaws eventually.'

"These minor things acceptable in job, after all labor job not flawless. Whatever rectification possible, I do but some of this means additional expense. You explain sir that work is done, and to release money after I finish small repair jobs. Ok?" Rajesh requested.

Rachna's quality checks were stringent and inflexible, she explained, "Sorry Rajesh, you will have to rectify this job completely. Whatever needs to be scrapped and built anew has to be done so and I'll get your payments sanctioned only after I see the complete job mended."

"But Rachna, labor job not always perfect. Anyways after completion these will not be seen," imposed Rajesh.

"Sorry, I want to see a properly done job before I can pay you."

"I will require money or work cannot progress," Rajesh was trying the fear psychosis on her. Rachna had such similar conversations with other contractors in the past and knew exactly how to handle them. Every consultant has a small kingdom of his own which he rules like a king. He also has his loyal subjects, who are continuously trying to prove that they are better than the rest to acquire maximum number of jobs to their credit. This eagerness of contractors to work with designers, which a common man doesn't earn, is what I call competition and it makes us, the designers, efficient. Rachna was well aware that Rajesh's statement was not to be replied to verbally. She made a call to one of our loyal contractors-Dinesh, "Dinesh, I want you to start a site which some other contractor has left mid-way. Come with your team over here in one hour maximum. I am texting the site address to you. Dinesh, no later than an hour." As she hung up the phone, she finished sending her text message and then turned to Rajesh, "Please wind up your tools and equipment. Since you can't work, I am getting someone else to complete the job properly." The fear psychosis had now reversed. Rajesh made a frantic call to me, "Sir, Rachna on site here, there are minor finishing errors for which she is asking me to close site."

"Rajesh, I told you before also, Rachna's call is final," I spoke casually. "Do as she instructs, otherwise it'll get difficult for you to work with us."

I disconnected the call, confident that Rajesh would now follow Rachna's orders. I looked at my phone to ensure it disconnected and I smiled when I re-read Rachna's message sent to me before I received Rajesh's call, "Rajesh acting tough, need to straighten him." I messaged back, "Job done?" to which I promptly received her reply, "Spoke to Dinesh in front of him, but have not messaged the address to him. Was sure Rajesh will straighten up after a threat. ☺"

Rachna sternly emphasized as she left the site, "Rajesh, I want this work rectified perfectly well before I get your next payment released. I will personally supervise this site, so no shortcuts. If at any stage you feel you aren't capable enough to do it up to my standards, then walk out and I'll get it completed by someone else." She then stared at him in the eye with her final remark, "You'll rectify at your expense. And I assure you, I'll ensure it. Nothing less than perfection is our standard." Rajesh only stared back at her in anger and hatred. He had been put down by his once-upon-a-time junior and had been overpowered beyond his reach.

He remembered the support that I had extended to him when he had authority, and now Rachna was enjoying the same confidence. I was always there to shield her. He needed to work with Dessign7 irrespective of whether or not his ego accepted Rachna's superiority. As Rachna was leaving the site, he recalled my cautionary remark, "If you had shown a little more patience, you would be in her position today." Rajesh looked at the closing door, hurt and with a tear of regret in his eyes. During the following week, he rectified all the errors at Mrs. Deol's site, at his cost. He invited Rachna for another site visit to check the rectification. After she was satisfied with the workmanship, she gave me her approval and I released Rajesh's next payment installment.

After the incident at Mrs. Deol's site, Rachna came up with a practical solution to prevent any of the franchisees to produce substandard quality work in the future. One day, whilst we were in the office, she suggested, "Sir, designing has always been our forte and with set management systems we can handle innumerous projects. Agreed?"

"Yes," I had to agree considering our design head was making the claim.

"We want to off load the site execution of our turnkey projects to the franchisees, due to our time constraints, otherwise we have already developed a strong network of vendors and contractors?" Rachna continued ending with a rhetorical question. "Neither by agreement nor by commitment are we bound to off load projects to the franchisees, right?" asked Rachna, this time awaiting my answer.

"Very good! So you finally cracked the franchise agreement and understood the concept," I quipped.

"Oh please, Sir! I am serious," Rachna said, reminding me of the exclamatory remark made by Palak. I wondered if these words were a part of their curriculum.

"We are not bound to out source sites to them. Our commitment is to support them with our profile and brand name; to provide them with training, designing and any technical assistance that they require. They are supposed to do their own client sourcing and sales. We are off loading sites to them because of our work load. What do you have in mind?" I asked eager to hear her idea.

"Instead of subcontracting the complete site to the mon a turnkey basis, we could only out source supervision to them for a supervision fee. That way, we'll have complete control over the material used and the quality of workmanship. We can pay for material and labor directly. Because the franchisee will not be investing any of his money, his profits will be reduced, controlling our overheads on the project. The profits that a franchisee makes on a project will also be more transparent. Also, our laborers know the standard of workmanship we require. The franchisee will only ensure co-ordination between various agencies and will be responsible for executing the entire project, as per the drawings, on time."

"Great idea! Today, for the first time in 5 years, I have felt that you are smart. Why didn't you use your brains all these years? I was going to ask you to put it for sale on OLX." I joked only to see Rachna grin, but indeed agreed that it was an ingenious, cost-saving, time-saving and quality-saving idea. Also, it was a good evolution of our initial concept. I continued becoming serious, "Rajesh is the one executing maximum sites at the moment. Let him complete those sites as per the contract and inform him that we'll adopt this new model for all future sites. Gauge his reactions. I would have spoken to him but since it's your idea, I want you to take the initiative!" Rachna smiled at my approval of her idea.

Rachna called Rajesh to the office the very next day. She explained the entire concept to Rajesh and waited for his reaction. "Rachna your idea or sir's idea?" Rajesh asked, clearly upset with this new concept.

"Actually my idea. Regarding the fiasco that happened at Mrs. Deol's site, I agree with you. Why should you bear the cost of any rectification because of a laborer's mistake? So, instead of bearing losses in training new laborers for Dessign7-approved workmanship standard, you can use existing labor contractors to execute the site. We also have pre-negotiated rate contracts with them. I have even spoken to the suppliers and they are willing to co-ordinate with you directly for material supply and raise the bill directly to us, with the usual credit period. You can decide your site supervision fees directly with sir." Rachna explained the advantages to Rajesh.

"Rachna, just because of one incident at Mrs. Deol, doesn't mean my work quality is bad. I also rectified that to your standard. You checked it also. I have been part of Dessign7 before, so I know the quality sir likes. It'll not happen again," Rajesh spoke defensively.

"Rajesh, I know you have been a part of Dessign7, but now it's grown to Dessign7 Interiors Pvt Ltd. The company has upgraded. The quality of designs, workmanship and etcetera have all been upgraded," Rachna spoke calmly.

"Rachna it's difficult to co-ordinate that way. My team will listen to me. Your team will not listen to me," Rajesh pointed out the disadvantage of the scheme.

"I understand your inhibition Rajesh, but I have spoken to them and they are all willing to work with you. As far as working comfort is concerned, you shouldn't have a problem with that because after you left Dessign7, you yourself had offered sites to them. But even then I will instruct them to listen to you."

"And what if suppliers don't give material on time and site gets delayed because of them?"

"Their deliveries have never faltered in years. Plan it well and place an order with them at least two days in advance and you'll never have a problem."

"But what is wrong with the current system?" Rajesh was getting agitated with Rachna's proposal. He knew that if he only got a supervision fee, his turnover per site would reduce drastically. The transparent working model proposed by Rachna would eat into his profit. Rachna understood his reservations, but her loyalties lay with Dessign7. She was doing what was best for the company.

"No Rachna, this will not do, I'll speak to sir!" Rajesh exclaimed.

"No point speaking to him. Other franchisees have already agreed to this model," Rachna bluffed. Rajesh was the only franchisee that she had spoken to.

"This is just not acceptable," Rajesh shouted, and marched straight into my cabin, "Sir, Rachna told me now you'll not sub-contract the job, only give supervision fees for executing job on time. It's all become chaos. It'll not work."

"Rajesh, let's try it for a few sites. If it doesn't work we'll go back to the old style of working. She's proposing this for the benefit of the company. Don't you want the company to benefit?" I asked him calmly, knowing that the answer was obvious. Rajesh calmed down, well aware that the decision was final. He shrugged his shoulders and agreed to try out the new model. As he walked out, he mentally marked Rachna as the person responsible for his losses. But he continued to work with Dessign7 with the same enthusiasm, waiting for the day that Rachna would falter.

Soon all tempers were pacified between the old and the new 'R's of Dessign7. Loud friction never happened again between them. Rajesh was still generating good revenue with this new model he had signed up for. Rachna was well experienced by now in governing contractors. Although sparks never flew, there was always an underlying tension waiting to erupt. Rajesh always wanted to prove his worthiness for the position that Rachna occupied, but Rachna was too seasoned to falter now. I preferred to ignore the underlying tension between them, provided it didn't surface again. If it did surface, I knew how to counsel them. In the meanwhile, I focused on our next step of evolution.

Rachna's work load pertaining to site execution was partially reduced, as some of the sites were off loaded to the new franchisees. Her new role was more managerial and to ensure smooth overall supervision. I was trying to gradually get her out of day-to-day site management. The idea was to expedite the process of evolution by off loading site execution and getting Rachna to be more involved with marketing, sales and overall management of the Pune office. This would leave me with sufficient time to expand to alternate cities. That was the next strategy of growth for our ever-evolving company.

Rachna started getting involved in marketing and sales and started jointly monitoring Zeenat's performance as well. She counselled Zeenat on ways to improve her sales efficiency and even started to observe my sales pitches to new clients to improve her own. Zeenat's performance in sales was improving and we had started getting fruitful results. Rachna's share of sales meetings with prospective clients was increasing and it was not long before she finalized her first contract with Mr. Vijay Kamthe.

The butterfly had soared a little higher.

Life's Crest and Trough 12

Zeenat had fixed an appointment with Mr. Vijay Kamthe, an inquiry that had come to Anagha. The inquiry had been passed on to Zeenat for follow-up and she ensured that the client came to the office for the initial presentation. Rachna attended to him. She delivered the presentation exactly the way we had penned it down in our training manual. She informed him in depth about our ISO-certified design and execution process, the time frame required for the site completion and the estimate of the project as per the requirements described by him. After she completed her presentation, Mr. Kamthe voiced his two major concerns, "Rachna, I liked the kind of work you have done and you appear to be a very systematic and professional company, but I find the costing too high and we'll need to move in much faster."

"Sir, our strength is our ISO-certified processes. There could be many other designers in the market whom you could consider awarding your job, but check whether they are ISO certified. If not, they would probably promise you a cheaper product in much lesser time, but they would not offer the service and guarantee that we offer. We give a genuine, written ten-year guarantee for all the works done by us. When you are going to spend so much on your dream home, you would at least expect it to last you for ten years. Any other company does not even offer a five-year guarantee and those who will give you that will be much more expensive than us. You can cross check that. We believe in the product we make for you.

"Your second issue was time. We track our site execution with the help of a detailed bar-chart, especially prepared for every site. If you want I can back track on the bar-chart and prove to you that the site can't be completed any faster. Renovating a home involves a lot of intricate designing and execution work. No two pieces of furniture have the same detailing and therefore it takes time to execute it. If it was an office project with repetitive workstations, we could have done it much faster, but home designing doesn't work that way. Other companies will promise you an earlier deadline initially, but later on as the work progresses, they'll stretch their schedule and you'll have no control over it. You'll be stuck. We on the other hand assure you that there will not be even a single-day delay in the schedule promised to you. You can plan your shifting in well ahead of time.

"I'll give you phone numbers of a few of our past clients and you can ask them about their experience of working with us and also about our after sales service," Rachna used a few confidence-building lines that I usually used, to conclude my presentation.

Rachna browsed through her iphone and gave names and numbers of three of our satisfied clients to Mr. Kamthe. He thanked Rachna for the presentation and he left the office with our brochure and Rachna's business card in his hand with the assurance that he would revert at the earliest. As it normally happens, a client raises an enquiry at least two months prior to him needing our services, so a constant follow-up is required during this period before he either assigns the job to us or refuses our services. Mr. Kamthe was impressed with Rachna's presentation and after the initial gestation period, he called Rachna and asked her to collect the nominal earnest money and begin with the design process. She was excited about finalizing her first contract, as she dashed into my cabin, "Sir, Mr. Vijay Kamthe finalized and is giving the advance tomorrow."

"Good, so you closed your first client. Really proud of you. You have grown well here and I don't only mean in size," I added a dash of humor. But honestly,the pride of a mentor when they see their students ecstatically succeed is supreme.

Rachna surveyed the site and began designing Mr. Kamthe's home. Sequential approvals were sought on drawings and the final estimate. As per our procedure the next lot of payments would come only once the work commenced on site and this was usually post the design process was complete and we had an approval on the entire design set. Mr. Kamthe was very happy as he approved the final design set. We were now to wait for a month before he would get the possession of his home and we could start our work.

In the meantime, Rachna finalized her second client, Mr. Prasad Singh. He appointed us to do the fit-out of his upcoming computer learning center. After we received his earnest money, we started working on the designs. Being a commercial premise, designing the aesthetics of his place was a lot simpler. Single units of the workstations and partitions had to be designed and then repeated multiple times as per the finalized layout. The designs had to be kept simple and monotonous to maintain uniformity throughout the office. However, it took tedious working hours to get the entire set of the technical working drawings prepared. Accurate and coordinated air conditioning, electrical and computer networking drawings were prepared by Vaishali and checked by Rachna. These were discussed with Mr. Singh and after incorporating the minor changes suggested by him, we finally received his approval. Alas, after a hectic fortnight, the designing phase was complete. Immediately after the designs were finalized, Rachna asked him for the mobilization advance. He said, "I am expecting some funds to be transferred by Monday, so after that you can collect your cheque on Wednesday. Is that fine?"

"Well, if you could release the cheque earlier, it would help me start the work faster. We are pressed for time, you understand," Rachna emphasized on 'pressed for time', making Mr. Singh realize that every passing day was precious to him.

"I know!" he agreed, "In that case, have your cheque collected on Monday itself. I'll make some arrangement."

"I'll call you on Monday morning." Rachna shook hands with him and concluded the meeting. As soon as Mr. Singh left, Rachna dialed 307 on the intercom and informed me elatedly, "Mr. Prasad Singh has approved all the drawings and he'll give the mobilization advance on Monday. Yaiyee!"

Rachna's passion for learning and putting her knowledge to practice had surpassed my expectation. She had not only proved herself to be a good designer and a technical head, but also a good business developer with superb acumen for business growth. Proud of her success, I personally designed a "Certificate of Appreciation", which was embossed with the company seal and signed by Anagha and me, both the directors of the company. We presented the same to her the very next morning with Anagha's congratulatory speech, "Rachna, you started your career in Dessign7 as a fresher and over the time you have displayed a huge penchant for learning and also putting that knowledge to productive use. You've grown a lot in this company and because of your loyalty and inputs even the company has grown a lot. You have excelled as a designer, technical manager and now even made your mark in business development. We are very proud of you." As she handed over the certificate to Rachna, she concluded, "And, this is just a way of appreciating your efforts."

Rachna stared at the certificate in disbelief, knowing very well that she was the second person in Dessign7 to have received this honor, only after Aaisha. She was striving to achieve this since long, but our raised bar was finally conquered. The joy of closing her second client was further exemplified with the receipt of this coveted certificate. It started a stream of tears from her eyes. Beneath a pretentious tough exterior that she portrayed to battle her professional life, still existed a warm person, well-touched by emotions. She spontaneously hugged Anagha tightly to display gratitude and as she wiped her tears, she shook my hand in affection,smiling ear to ear. She was lost for words, but her fumbled expressions spoke paragraphs. I, on the contrary, had only one thing to say, "Rachna, don't cry so much! The maid has just mopped the floor and it'll get all wet again."

Very theatrically, she grinned and rushed out of the cabin before a fresh flood of tears broke loose. It was a good gesture. In fact, I was sure it was a great gesture to end her week with a new crest. She called me a few minutes later, on the intercom, asking if she could take the rest of the day off. She was eager to share the joy with her family. I obviously granted the request and she left office early, smiling away to success. Of course, an occasional tear did make its way as she shared the joy with her family.

But then tears of joy are always welcome.

***

In the afternoon, as I returned from my site visit, I saw Rajesh waiting at the reception. I inquired with him the purpose for his visit. He said, "Rachna called me to explain Mr. Garg's drawings - that new client. She said site to be started soon."

"Rachna is not coming back for the day. Did you call her before coming?" I asked.

"Yes, she said Vaishali has drawings and she'll explain it. I am waiting for her," Rajesh replied.

"Zeenat, have you informed Vaishali that Rajesh is waiting?" I asked her and I went into my cabin, not waiting for her reply.

Vaishali came to the waiting lobby and Rajesh followed her into the studio to discuss the drawings. Vaishali had already received her instructions from Rachna regarding all the issues that would need clarification. It was a brief meeting after which they were waiting for the printouts of the final set, to be given to Rajesh. Vaishali asked him, "I hope you've understood all the drawings."

"Yes, you explain very well. You also make this design yourself?" asked Rajesh.

"Yes, smaller projects are handled by me independently," Vaishali spoke proudly.

"I see your designing is good. How long you been here with Dessign7?"

"I have been here almost two years now. I believe you were working here a few years ago. I think before Rachna ma'am had joined," Vaishali was trying to recollect the gossip that she had heard from Zeenat.

"Yes, I was Rachna's boss. I trained her," Rajesh said pompously. "But two years is long time and your designing also good. You take independent sites on your own?"

"No, not at all!" Vaishali was on her guard.

"We used to do own sites, maybe even Rachna must be doing own sites. No wonder she must have gone early today," Rajesh paused to allow that comment to sink in.

"Forget that, but now you should do own site side by side, otherwise how you progress?"

"But that is cheating sir and ma'am, both."

"Not really, sir also understands. In this line, everyone does their own site after one or two years. Then eventually they partner with someone who can handle sites well and they start own business. I can handle site well, but my designer-cum-partner, Aaron is planning to shift to Aurangabad, so I am finding good designer. Let me know if you have someone in mind – some college friend or batch mate."

"When did you start taking your own site? Whilst you were still working at Dessign7 or after you left office?" Vaishali was now intrigued.

"When I was working here, I started my own sites. There were some clients who wanted small jobs done which sir not interested in. So those jobs I took directly and execute them. That's OK because sir anyways not going to take them. So, this way I am also happy, even client happy with work because of we give slightly cheaper and no loss to company also. You should also try."

"No it'll not work with me. I know about designing, but I still have a lot to learn about costing, dealing with clients, etcetera."

"Don't worry about that, I teach you. If you have any project, let me know. You can design and I manage everything else. We'll divide profit fifty-fifty." Rajesh said winding up the discussion, as his printouts were ready.

"I'll let you know if anything comes," Vaishali said curtly, in an attempt to halt the discussion. Something about Rajesh's offer didn't appeal to her conscience.

"You'll do designing for me if I get a site?" Rajesh asked Vaishali directly.

Vaishali thought about his offer, analyzing whether her moral values would permit her to accept the offer. After a long pause, she finally spoke, "Yes I will do the designing for you." Rajesh impatiently, started smiling at the acceptance of his offer, instead of waiting for Vaishali to finish her statement. Vaishali continued, "But only if it comes to me officially through Dessign7. Not otherwise, and next time if you make such an offer to anyone in the office, I'll have to report it to Rachna ma'am."

A long silence followed and multiple looks were exchanged. Vaishali's offensive looks made Rajesh realize that he had approached the wrong kind of person with his proposal. Rajesh's regretful looks conveyed his apology to Vaishali. Finally the tension broke when Rajesh took the drawing set apologetically and quietly walked out of the office.

Rajesh appreciated Vaishali's loyalty and honesty. However, for Vaishali, he had triggered her thoughts. She spent the next few days evaluating the alternate career path shown by Rajesh. She started wondering whether an alliance with Rajesh would be a way to fast-track her career. She was assessing the feasibility of his proposal.

***

"We need to collect the mobilization advance from Mr. Prasad Singh. If he doesn't call by this afternoon, then you call him," was my early Monday morning reminder to Rachna. Later in the day Rachna called him, "Hi, this is Rachna from Dessign7. When can I send someone to collect the advance?"

"Well there is a change in plan. The institute whose franchisee we had taken for the computer center says that we'll have to use their vendor for the fit-out. So we might not be going ahead with this project, but I want to refurbish my house shortly so I will get in touch with you for that. Thanks." With this information, he abruptly terminated the contract, wasting our fortnight's effort.

A dejected Rachna informed me of the conversation which concluded with the loss of a project, to which I explained, "Defeats are that important part of a business without which our victories will not be dear. We eventually learn to take in our stride. It's possible that he tricked us into designing the project for him and found some small timer to give him a cheaper quote to execute the job. After all,our expertise lies is in the designs he got from us." She appreciated the philosophy, but it was only natural for her to grieve her first defeat.

As soon as Rachna was out of the cabin, she spoke to Zeenat, "Did Mr. Singh call you, or did you call him?"

"No! You never asked me to call him, did you?" Zeenat replied with another question.

"No I didn't but I was just checking if you spoke to him after we last met."

"There was no reason to speak to him. I have not called him!" Zeenat said, categorically indicating that her job doesn't require her to speak to the client after he has awarded the project to us.

Rachna went to the studio and asked Vaishali, "Did you mail Mr. Prasad's drawings to him?"

"Yes ma'am. On Friday itself," she replied, proud of her efficiency.

"He cancelled the contract. Did you speak to him after his meeting that day?"

"No! He was happy with the designs that day. He even approved them. Why did he terminate the contract? Did he find the costing high?" Vaishali asked looking surprised.

"No, he said because of some company policy, he had to use another agency." Rachna answered, lost in her own thoughts, trying to figure out the reason for the loss of that project. Suddenly, she wondered why Vaishali brought up the costing issue. She pondered on her question for a while but eventually, she got involved with other work at hand. Subconsciously, a question was still bothering Rachna, 'Why did Vaishali bring up the cost issue?'

****

The next few days were much brighter, and even the weather favored our uplifted moods. Interior works of Mrs. Deol's bungalow were almost complete, only the final finishing touches were remaining. Every passing day, wall papers and curtains of various areas were being installed. Rachna kept receiving excited calls from Mrs. Deol appreciating the way each room was turning out. Her excitement encouraged us to make additional site visits just to see and enjoy the outcome of our efforts. Rachna's quality checks on Rajesh's work ensured that we ended up with good quality work, on par with Dessign7 standards. We usually put in months of efforts to complete a project, stressing ourselves to the maximum, but all of it seems worth it when the final, finished product is appreciated by the client. As a designer, I can clearly visualize the finished space even before the work has started, but seeing the end product always thrills me. And the happy smile on Mrs. Deol's excited face was the icing on the cake.

Another happy client couple was Sneha and Anand. It had been a while since they had shifted into their four-bedroom bungalow, but owing to their prior commitments, they never had an official housewarming party. So, they held a lavish dinner for a few friends and relatives. Obviously, they invited us – the stars of the evening. Anagha, Rachna and I attended the function. Anand personally introduced us to most of his guests, who congratulated us on designing their beautiful home. 'Simple', 'elegant', 'contemporary' were some words used by most guests to describe our designing style. I enjoyed the attention and basked in the glory of our creation. We also received a lot of references of Anand's friends who were contemplating renovating their houses in the near future.

Two satisfied and appreciating clients contributed to ending our week on a high note. But like how every crest rises after a trough, it is even followed by a trough. That's a periodic business cycle.

***

A week later, Rachna called up Mr. Kamthe for the keys to his apartment and the mobilization advance. Mr.Kamthe disconnected the call and sent her a text message reading, "Rates u quoted too high, getting work done by other person. Thanks." Rachna was shattered. Her success cycle was going through a trough again with both her celebrated victories converting to defeats. She sat paralyzed at her desk for a few minutes trying to absorb the message, unsure as to how to break the news to me. She even sent a return message to him "Can you please mail the quote to me? I can compare it and revert to you with any anomalies". This was a procedural request we often made to a negotiating client at the pitching stage of a project. Firstly, it verified if the client had genuinely received a lesser quote or was it his strategy for negotiating our rates. Secondly we could make an apple-to-apple comparison of our quote versus the lower quote that the client received. Competitors often reduced cost by using inferior specifications. Mr.Kamthe replied back saying, "Too late, we have already started work with him." The discussion had ended.

Rachna had flashes of images going through her mind. It was only a couple of weeks ago that she had very proudly accepted the "Certificate of Appreciation", and now the very reason for earning that certificate didn't exist. There were two clients to her credit. Both clients were lost. Losing a finalized client was more disheartening than the joy of closing the two clients in the first place. She was mentally rehearsing how she would break the news to me and with the same confusion in her head, she walked into my cabin, placed the certificate on the table in front of me and broke into tears as she started to speak, "I don't think I deserve this certificate." I was trying to hear the words between the sobs and after a little persuasion, I was enlightened of the reason for returning the certificate.

"Mr. Kamthe messaged and even he's getting his place done by someone else. We lost his project, too. Both the clients I had finalized are gone." She was desperately trying to wipe the tears rolling down her cheeks.

"What?!? Are you kidding me? How can we lose two clients in a fortnight? It has never happened before that a client is lost out at such advanced stages of design. We've spent a lot of time and effort behind these guys. What's Kamthe's reason?" I asked, shocked at the loss.

"He said he's getting a cheaper quote."

"Cheaper by how much? Ask him to come to the office for a discussion or ask him to mail the quote. Tell him we'll compare it apple-to-apple and revert to him."

"Already did that. He refused to send the quote saying that he has already got the work commenced."

"Why don't you go and investigate who is working on that site and whether they are also using our designs? It'll not help us regain the project but at least we'll be more aware of who our competitors are."

"I'll do that. Will check it up," she spoke, still wiping the tears off her face and slid the certificate towards me, "I don't think I deserve this."

"Rachna, this certificate was given to you for your continuous efforts in Dessign7 since the last five years. Don't let an odd incident upset you. Mrs. Deol and Anand are very happy with the places that you have designed for them. Ups and downs are a part of any business. Don't let them deject you so much. You very much deserve this certificate and you have to keep it."

"No sir, not today. Keep this certificate with you today and next when you feel that I truly deserve it, I'll accept it."

"Fine. This will await you here." I said hesitatingly as I locked the certificate in a safe drawer.

"I am sure you'll soon find an occasion to earn it again. By the way, go to Kamthe's site and check who's working there."

Rachna's dejection was evident for the rest of the day. Even the staff noticed and enquired about it, but she shrugged it off. She sat alone in her cubicle wondering what went wrong with Mr. Kamthe's project. She recalled every meeting with him, running in her mind every bit of conversation that she remembered to have exchanged with him. She couldn't remember him being dissatisfied with any of the designs finalized. So, it must be our quote that he must have found high. He did confirm that through his message.

Rachna recollected Mr. Singh's project. That project had also followed the same pattern. Both the clients were happy interacting with Rachna throughout the sales pitch and design finalization, but both projects were lost prior to commencement. She wondered whether costing was their genuine concern. She had shared the ballpark estimate of the project even before receiving their earnest money, and they were alright with the estimate. That's the reason that they finalized with Dessign7 in the first place. Then Rachna recalled Vaishali's question, at the time of losing Mr. Singh's project. She had asked whether they found the costing high. Rachna asked herself, "How did she arrive at the thought that the costing was high? Why did she ask that question?"Rachna was continuously repeating these questions to herself and eventually the stress gave her a splitting headache. She sought my permission to take the rest of the day off, as she didn't have any client meeting lined up for the day. Knowing the stress she was going through, I granted her the same.

The next day, Rachna had emotionally stabilized a little. She was still dismayed about the loss of her two projects, but realized that other sites required her attention. She went through the day completing her daily responsibilities. Rajesh came to the office that afternoon to clarify a few doubts he had about Mr. Garg's site. Rachna didn't have the heart to hassle with Rajesh, so she requested Vaishali to discuss the queries with him. Rajesh was surprised at Rachna's absence from the meeting. He quickly asked Vaishali, "What happen? Rachna not joining meeting?"

"No, she's busy with some other work," Vaishali answered.

"Didn't look like she was too busy. Anyways," Rajesh said and proceeded with his list of doubts. After discussing all the points, Vaishali offered solutions to most of the queries. For a few cost-affecting issues that she wasn't authorized to decide on, she summarized the points for Rachna and sought her decision. Rachna was pre-occupied with her thoughts, but carefully listened to Vaishali, ensuring not to miss out on any important point. After Vaishali finished her brief, Rachna gave her a clearance on all of the points and asked Vaishali to convey the decision to Rajesh. Just as Vaishali turned to leave her cubicle, Rachna said, "Before you give the clearance to Rajesh, check it with sir once."

Vaishali excused herself into the cabin and said, "Sir, there were a few doubts that Rajesh had regarding Mr. Garg's site, so I just wanted to clarify some cost-related issues with you."

I was reading an important legal document, as I looked up and said, "I am slightly busy. Ask Rachna to take a look at it." I returned to my documents.

"She's already seen it, but wants you to give a final okay," Vaishali insisted that I approve.

"If Rachna has approved it, go ahead with it," I said, trusting Rachna's decision.

"Fine sir, then I'll give the approval to Rajesh," she said, leaving the cabin and closing the door behind her.

Rajesh got his approvals and on his way out, he opened the cabin door slightly, popped his head inside and asked, "You free for few minutes? I want to discuss something with you."

"I am slightly busy now. I need to finish going through these documents and I need to reply to it today itself. Can you come in the morning tomorrow?" I asked him, preoccupied with the papers in front of me.

"Fine, I'll come by 10:30 tomorrow," Rajesh said and he left the office.

I will always remember that day as an unpleasant one. As it was, I was unhappy about the loss of two clients in such a short span of time. Additionally, I was trying to concentrate on the important documents in front of me, but I was constantly being disturbed by people walking into the cabin. Also, Rachna was losing her confidence that day, owing to her own downheartedness. She came to the cabin a couple of times, to take my consent on a few minor decisions she was issuing on site. She was well aware of her authority to take those decisions on her own, but I could sense extra precaution in her questions. Although I was preoccupied with my own agenda, I tried to motivate her, but in vain. I perfectly understood her inability to accept failure. I sympathized with her, but honestly speaking, anyone in her situation would be shook up. She had perpetually proved herself as a technical manager but after these incidents, I was unsure of her as business development manager. At that vulnerable moment, I wanted Rachna to avoid any sales meetings with prospective clients. I felt that a negative response would only demoralize her further.

I recalled that Rachna was scheduled to meet a new client that evening. I spoke to Zeenat to confirm, "Was a new client supposed to come for a meeting today?"

"Yes sir, Mr. Amaresh, he is supposed to meet Rachna ma'am at five o'clock."

"What are the details of his property?" I inquired.

"He has a three-bedroom penthouse at Wakad. He is an NRI and wants to finalize immediately."

"I am going to be in office today. Divert that client to me. I'll keep myself free in the evening," I said, trying to sound as casual as possible. I was wondering how I would possibly finish reading and replying to the documents that were demanding my undivided attention since morning with this added responsibility.

"Even I think that's better sir. Anyway we have lost both the clients that Rachna ma'am had finalized, so at this stage let's not take the chance." We had a close-knit office and advanced communication technology is slower than the rate at which information travels verbally in such a setup. Zeenat was bound to gauge the reason for a change in the meeting schedule.

"If Rachna asks for a reason for the changed schedule, ask her to speak to me," I spoke softly to Zeenat, revealing my anxiety to her. Zeenat conveyed my decision to

Rachna. Although unhappy with my decision, Rachna never questioned me. She understood.

My meeting with Mr. Amaresh was fruitful. He had already seen our website and was impressed with our designing style. Since he had come with the intent of finalizing with us, it was a short meeting to understand our method of working and the estimate for the interiors. He had already studied the market and had various proposals from other designers, so he made an immediate decision. He concluded the meeting by handing over a cheque for the earnest money and requested us to start the designing immediately. Finalizing with a new client was definitely a good way to end an otherwise unpleasant day.

In the evening, Rachna informed me of her decision to go to Mr. Kamthe's site the following morning to investigate who was working on the site. She preferred to go directly from home as it was closer. She inquired with me if I would join her for the visit, but I declined as I had already scheduled a meeting with Rajesh. Anyway there was only post-mortem to be conducted on site to investigate who our competitor was.

The project was already lost.

Expanding Horizon 13

The next morning Rajesh was already waiting for me at the reception, chatting with Zeenat, as I entered the office. After exchanging pleasantries with both of them, I invited Rajesh to the cabin. I was still preoccupied with the two vanished clients and the dismay showed on my face. Also, I was concerned because of the stress that Rachna was undergoing.

"What happened, you sad?" questioned Rajesh. Rajesh could read me like a book. He recognized my every expression. He could distinguish between my quietness and sadness. However, the question could have also been a product of Rajesh and Zeenat's early morning chit-chat.

"Yes, I am a little worried. Last month Rachna had finalized two clients and we lost both of them. This has never happened in the history of Dessign7. We might have lost clients before at pitching stage but we have never lost clients after finalization," was my honest confession to Rajesh. After all, he was almost family.

"Yes that never happen before. Maybe Rachna can't deal properly with client. She can handle designing but not overall manage."

"That's not possible. She managed to finalize two projects, so the sales pitch was alright. But I can't figure out why we lost the clients," I was thinking aloud.

Rajesh spoke slowly, carefully selecting his words and allowing time for them to sink in, "Maybe she not explain the quotation to them properly. That's why we lose them. I never think that Rachna can manage the way you and I used to manage. I think she is too much theory and no practical. You know how I managed Nashik. And then I got lots of projects also in Nashik. Now I am even more experienced. If you want help to look after clients, let me know. I always there for you."

I realized that I had created an opportunity for Rajesh to criticize Rachna, which he was making the most of. Without further discussing the topic, I came to the agenda of our meeting, "So, you wanted to speak to me about something?"

"Yes! We want to give franchise in Aurangabad?" Rajesh asked.

"Of course we can give a franchise in Aurangabad. We'll obviously have to evaluate the credentials of the franchisee, but we are definitely interested in giving a franchise in there. Someone you know is interested?" I asked enthusiastically.

"Yes. You know AaronJames, that Hallmark guy? You also know we do some projects with each other. He is planning to shift and live in Aurangabad. He wants our franchise for Aurangabad." I knew Aaron fairly well and always regarded him as an average designer, but if trained well, he could prove to be an asset to Dessign7. I also knew that Rajesh allied with him for various projects, even whilst he was working with Dessign7, and was sure that he must have briefed Aaron thoroughly on the working style of Dessign7.

"That's great. Aurangabad is progressing quite well and it's a good place to have some market share. Anyone in Aurangabad wanting to do premium project normally hires an interior designer from Pune or Mumbai. They know we are exposed to the latest trends in designing. If we have an execution office there, we'll become the preferred choice of such premium clients because we'll be able to offer them daily supervision which other designers in Mumbai and Pune can't give. Did you explain to him the entire model, franchise fee, etcetera?"

This news uplifted my mood. Aurangabad was an upcoming town, around a five-hour drive from Pune, with good business prospects. Also, adding another branch to Dessign7 was definitely an exciting proposal.

"You send agreement draft to him by mail. He'll go through it and next week he's in Pune for some work so we sign the agreement then," saying this, Rajesh messaged Aaron's phone number and email ID to me, which I acknowledged with a nod. I smiled at him to appreciate his newfound marketing skills, "Thanks Rajesh, you have always proved to be an asset to Dessign7. And I can see now that your marketing skills are improved tremendously. I am proud and happy that you are back on board."

"I don't mind coming back full time, if you want. I can handle marketing for new clients and for franchising. Let Rachna handle the designing and technical part and I will focus on getting new projects. We both on par managing different departments." Rajesh was quick in converting my compliment to an offer.

"You mean to say that you want to join Dessign7 again, full time?" I asked, not expecting him to agree.

"Yes, you pay me same salary plus incentive. The same way you pay Rachna. I will supervise Zeenat's calling, new client leads, closing clients, everything marketing related. Just like I used to do before leaving." Rajesh said with a grin.

"Well, if you are serious then let me think about it. I'll have to speak to Anagha and Rachna."

"You ask them. Anagha ma'am will have no problem, but Rachna will not like me joining. She's too afraid of me."

"Let me think about it," I said postponing the topic to a further date.

We were making general small talk and when Rachna walked in to tell me about her investigation, I waved a hand gesture to ask her to come in after sometime. As I was eager to learn the results of her findings, I cut short my conversation with Rajesh and bid him farewell. I thanked him for his effort once again.

Rajesh encountered Rachna in the reception instructing Zeenat to make a few phone calls and taking a follow-up for some of the clients she had met in the last few weeks. The incident was fresh on Rajesh's mind and he would never miss an opportunity to get back at Rachna.

"Zeenat, marketing and sales is job of experts. Pay attention and do well. Make sure you don't lose any clients otherwise Dessign7 will suffer your mistake. If you don't know, ask me. I'll teach you."

Rachna shot a glance at him. If looks could kill, Rajesh would be burning in hell. Rajesh had framed and directed his sentence well at Zeenat, who was only surprised at the intention of his remark. Rachna understood the comment but chose not to respond to it.

As soon as Rajesh left, Rachna entered the cabin to update me about the site visit. The work had started with a few carpenters working on site. The drawings that they were following were very similar to our designs but they were not using our exact designs. There were minor alterations. They have basically implemented all our concepts with minor tweaking. They have down sized the specification of plywood and finishing items to probably reduce the cost.

"He has hired a professional agency but I couldn't find out which. I asked the laborers on site but they didn't have a clue. They said that their main contractor would probably know the designer but the main contractor wasn't available on site.

"So we surely lost that job," I said,disappointed. "What about the drawings there, did you check the name on the drawings?"

"There was no phone number or company address on the drawing. It was prepared by some AJ & Associates," replied Rachna with a shrug.

"Anyway, let's forget about it. There is some good news," I said to change the mood, "Rajesh's friend wants to take our franchise for Aurangabad. He has been working with Rajesh for some time; now he's planning to shift to Aurangabad and wants to represent us over there. I think it'll be a good association. He's coming to Pune next week to sign the agreement," I said impatiently.

"Good. Very Good. What's his name?"

"Aaron. Aaron James. I think it was a very good idea to get Rajesh back in Dessign7, don't you think so?" I asked as Rachna got up to leave the cabin.

"Yes, it was a good idea to get him back," Rachna's voice faded out as she walked out of the cabin.

14 Best of Luck

The next week entailed routine work with site visit predominantly occupying most of our time. I decided to make a few site visits myself. Whenever Rachna was scheduled to make a site visit, I would accompany her to check the site progress from my perspective. Rachna's forte was to ensure that the designs were followed perfectly and any deviations from the drawings were rectified. I spent my time conducting random quality checks, inspecting material wastage and minor finishing details. I always believed that if you consistently look at the same problem day after day, you sometimes miss out the obvious solution. So a second opinion is very necessary. The precious time between the site visits was utilized to supervise Zeenat to improve her follow-up of new clients, and of course,to set up meetings with new clients. Since the previous week was still fresh on my mind, I had already instructed Zeenat to divert all new clients to Anagha and me only. Rachna was going through a temporary dip and I didn't want it to aggravate.

"Sir, there is an inquiry from a Tania Raghunathan. She has a 2BHK on B.T. Kawade Road. She wants to come for a meeting, but she had called with Rachna ma'am's reference so should I fix an appointment for you or Rachna ma'am?" asked Zeenat on Wednesday morning.

"Set up a meeting for me," I said; then added as an afterthought, "If she's called with Rachna's reference then ask Rachna if she'd like to handle it. When does she want to come?"

"This evening. I'll check if Rachna ma'am is free, I'll ask her to handle it or else I'll set it up for you," Zeenat closed the cabin door with the usual smile on her face. Her eagerness to set up the appointment was evident. She was on an incentive-based model and every appointment she successfully set meant an additional incentive in her forthcoming salary.

Rachna immediately grasped the opportunity to prove herself as good business developer. She enthusiastically agreed to meet the new client, even though it was fixed for late evening. She promptly took the client's number from Zeenat and even agreed to coordinate with her after office hours.

As I was leaving for home that evening, I walked out of my cabin to see a tall lady, in her late twenties, waiting at the reception. Dressed in a striped formal shirt and grey trousers, it was obvious that she had just returned from work. I raised a questioning eyebrow to Zeenat as I took a detour into the studio. Zeenat followed me and when she was clearly out of the stranger's sight she whispered, "Tania, the new client I told you about. 2BHK at B.T. Kawade Road. She's come to meet Rachna ma'am."

I recalled Zeenat mentioning her in the morning and looked towards Rachna, who was just rising from her seat to make her way to the reception to invite the client for a detailed presentation. As she crossed me I whispered, "Best of luck."

"Thanks, I need it now more than ever," she replied with fortitude. She had the eyes of a soldier making way for battlefield. I sincerely wished that she would successfully confirm this client's job, especially after the fiasco of the last two clients. It was required more to boost her confidence than for our financial need. Also, I was positive that Rachna would bag this client, as they were approximately the same age and they would vibe well. I left office for the day, leaving Rachna with her prospective client and my best wishes.

I started the next morning by inquiring with Rachna about her client meeting the previous day. "It was good, she'll most probably confirm today," she said and then turning to Zeenat she added, "She's asked to give a call today afternoon. She'll probably give the advance today itself. Call her between 1-2pm during her lunch break." Rachna appeared pleased. It seemed ages since I had seen Rachna feel optimistic again. I hoped that she would finalize Tania's project so that I could return her the certificate, which was patiently lying in my drawer, awaiting its true owner.

I spoke to Aaron that afternoon and fixed a meeting for the following Monday evening to sign the franchise agreement. He confirmed, "Can we meet at 5pm at your office? I have a site meeting in the morning? Also, I'll handover the cheque for the franchise fee at that time. I have gone through the draft and we just need to sign it, so we should be done in half an hour I guess."

"Yes, that seems fine. I will keep two copies of the agreement ready; we'll require witnesses so I'll also arrange for Rajesh to be here and we can ask Rachna and Zeenat from my office to be the other witnesses."

I called Rachna and Zeenat to the cabin and asked them to be present in office on Monday evening.

"AaronJames, the guy interested in taking a franchise for Aurangabad is coming down on Monday so you guys need to be in office at 5pm to sign as witnesses. Just ensure you don't plan any other meetings."

Rachna was busy fiddling with her phone and smiling away with a crafty look very unnatural of her. She agreed to be available for the evening session on Monday but asked for leave for some personal work on Monday morning. Obviously, I granted it.

The afternoon conversation with Aaron had left me with a high, only for my mood to decline in the evening. I was wondering why the 'periodic business cycle' was taking us so rapidly through its crests and troughs.

Zeenat informed me that Tania had decided to appoint someone else to design her home. She didn't state a reason but said that her decision was made. We had lost one more client attended by Rachna. I was confused as to whether she was having a phase of bad luck or whether she really was not meant for sales. In both the cases, I sympathized with her, but decided not to permit her to attend any new clients in the near future. In the evening, before I left for the day, I called her in the cabin and asked her, "Should we call Tania for another meeting, just to understand what the issue is? I am sure she must not have finalized with someone else so soon."

"No! Please don't!" she exclaimed, a little startled and then wished me goodbye, with the sly smile that was plastered on her face since morning.

Manic Monday 15

Monday arrived very soon. I had always felt that time flaps its wings like a butterfly, it leaves you with colorful memories but it also flutters away very fast. It felt like just yesterday when we were conceptualizing and creating our franchise program. Today, we were to sign up our seventh franchisee and our first franchise out of the city. Although it proposed to be a productive Monday, it was accompanied by the characteristic 'Monday morning blues'. The sound track "Manic Monday" had scarred me for life. After I heard that song, I could never visualize Monday as a pleasant day to return to work. It always started with the stressful recollection of all the work left pending during the previous week. I was already missing the relaxed Sunday that had gone by in blink. I failed to understand which equation of mathematics stated that one day of relaxing can equate to six days of work. Obviously, someone had got the math wrong. And just for the record, the ordeal of getting up and dragging oneself to work after a relaxing Sunday is something that even the boss of the company doesn't enjoy, a thought not popularly believed by his employees.

I started the day by asking Zeenat for the usual follow-up on the marketing calls made during the previous week. Whilst Zeenat was hunting for her data on the laptop, of which I could only see the back, I made a reminder-cum-confirmation call to Aaron for our meeting later in the evening. Upon receiving his confirmation, I sent a collective text message to Rachna, Rajesh and Anagha to be present in the office by five o'clock. I verbally informed Zeenat about requiring her presence in the evening, whilst she was deeply engrossed in searching through the calling list, making last minute updates to it. She acknowledged my request with a nod, and turned the laptop screen towards me. As I went through Zeenat's updated file on the laptop, she asked me a couple of new queries that some clients raised regarding our method of work. I gave her a detailed explanation to clear her doubts and also gave her short answers which she could give to clients. At the end of it, I insisted on a more rigorous follow-up to close some of the prospective clients that I had met. A motivated, "Yes sir, don't worry! I'll close them soon," from Zeenat concluded our meeting. It was a response I had heard multiple times before in the past, but it never followed a determined action. As she was leaving the cabin, I requested her to get two copies of the franchise agreement printed and franked for rupees one hundred, so that it could be signed and notarized today itself.

Rachna was absent for the pre-lunch session but she was, as usual, in touch with her basecamp. Her army of designers had already been assigned tasks to be accomplished throughout the day, and they were working well towards meeting their targets. Monday mornings are usually hectic because the previous week has to be summed up and the new week has to begin with great momentum to achieve a highly productive week. Realizing this well, it was quite unlike Rachna to take a break on Monday, but I trusted that it must be for something very urgent.

Anagha and I met Rachna during lunch, once she was back in office. As we set the table I extended courtesy, "Did you manage to finish off your work?" The sly smile was back on her face as she nodded in consent. All through the afternoon the reason for her smile eluded me.

Aaron and Rajesh walked into the office together at around 4:45 pm. Zeenat asked them to wait at the reception and informed me of their arrival. I quickly inquired the status of the agreement and when she confirmed that it was ready, I invited Aaron and Rajesh to the cabin. Zeenat led them in, and after placing the agreement on my table she excused herself. Aaron and Rajesh sat in front of Anagha and me. I pushed the document towards Aaron which he promptly picked up. Whilst he was browsing through the ten-page agreement, giving it a final check, the three of us indulged in some small talk. I gave an occasional glance towards him to look for any signs of doubt. It's interesting to notice that the ease with which people give verbal consent is inversely proportionate to the wrinkled lines of scrutiny on their faces whilst endorsing the same consent on paper. But I let Aaron take his time before we were finally prepared to sign the franchise deed.

Once Aaron had thoroughly read the agreement and was satisfied with it, I asked Rachna and Zeenat to join us for the meeting. I introduced them to Aaron and once the pleasantries, were exchanged, I offered a pen to both of them and asked them to sign the dotted line earmarked for witness. As Zeenat was about to sign,Rachna expressed a doubt, "Sir, I have a doubt before we sign the agreement."

My surprised expression could only speak, "Pardon?"

"Well sir, if Vaishali betrayed us, do you think it would be right for us to still have her in the office?" All eyes were now looking at the questioner, searching for its relevance in the current context.

"Rachna,why is this relevant now? And how did Vaishali cheat us? Why would she cheat us?!" I asked, puzzled with the appropriateness of her statements.

"No, what if Vaishali has been leaking important office information?"

"I don't think she'd do that." It was unbelievable that Vaishali, our young, loyal designer, whom we looked upon as a future core team member, would betray us.

"Again that can be discussed later. I don't see its relevance just now!"

"Oh but it is relevant, sir. The leaked information was delivered to someone in this room. And the information was leaked to sabotage our company. You should be aware of the facts before you sign up our new associate. He could be the culprit for all you know." She turned to the person in question, "Aaron, I believe you came to Pune this morning itself. Where were you since?"

"I had a few site meetings. And, what right do you have to ask me this in such a tone?" Replied Aaron offended by the way Rachna questioned him.

"What's the relevance of this question, Rachna? What culprit are you talking about?" I questioned, utterly confused and clueless about such behavior on her part, that too with a perfect stranger. But Rachna ignored me and continued speaking to Aaron.

"A few site meetings; or precisely two site meetings?" She asked with huge pauses,emphasizing on the figure two. Rachna turned to me and continued, "Mr. Aaron came from Aurangabad and coincidentally, made his first site visit at Mr. Prasad's site at precisely 10:30 am. My urgent work this morning was to welcome Mr. Aaron to Pune. Since 8:30 am in the morning, I had been waiting for Aaron outside Mr. Prasad's building. I had a hunch that he would visit there first as the site is closer once he enters Pune from Aurangabad. Only, I didn't know what time he was coming. Aaron you really shouldn't make a girl wait so much." Rachna flashed a sarcastic smile and continued, "It was a blind date, but it was worth a shot. I didn't recognize him at first, but who else, except the great AJ, would visit our site at such early morning hours? And that too to shamelessly execute our designs there. At 11:30 am he left for his second meeting and strangely enough I ended up following him to Mr. Kamthe's site. Voila! The mysterious AJ & Associates was none other than AaronJames and Associates. He obviously got a copy of our drawing sets from the respective clients, he forged them, then tweaked them a little and re-branded our designs under AJ & Associates.

"After reaching there at 12:15 pm, he spent precisely forty five minutes on site, to explain our stolen designs to the contractors. And I am sure with the exception of a few minutes here and there, Mr. Aaron will agree to this schedule. Right,Aaron? I have photographs on my phone of you entering and leaving both the sites. So, don't even dream of denying it!"

Aaron was bewildered at this revelation. My clarity of the situation increased as Aaron's silence grew.

"You are really stupid to use a phony name like 'AJ & Associates' to deceive us. You forget, that we are your seniors in this field!" was Rachna's closing remark.

"Aaron, you allied with Vaishali in my office. You allied with her to get numbers of our clients." I couldn't believe that this was happening to me. It was the kind of thing that I saw in movies only.

"Even our quotations were exposed to him and he purposely undercut us to bag these jobs," Rachna added.

I shouted, raising my pitch towards the end of the sentence, "And after all this you have the bloody guts to sit in front of me asking me for a franchise? You sly bastard! Previously you allied with Rajesh whilst he was working with me and now Vaishali? What a bastard!" I was growing angry and totally astounded by this revelation. "Where is Vaishali? Rachna, call her in immediately."

Rachna spoke calmly, "But sir, I said 'suppose' Vaishali was involved, I didn't say that Vaishali was involved. Vaishali interacts with a client only after we commence work on site. Who do you think in our office would have the complete data to sabotage our project post the marketing stage? Someone who has completed her interaction with the client, has got her incentive on the finalized client and still has the client details with her." And she turned to Zeenat. "Zeenat is the traitor who supplied client details to Aaron. Right, Zeenat?"

"No way sir, why would I do that? I swear I wouldn't do that," Zeenat defended herself. "I have been with Dessign7 for over seven years now and sir you also treat me like your sister. Why would I ever cheat you?"

"Zeenat, I don't know why you would cheat," continued Rachna, "but I do know that I found a strange phenomenon when I checked your personal phone the other day. Why don't you show it to sir, Zeenat?" as she quickly snatched the phone from Zeenat's hand and held it out to me. I took the phone from Rachna and focused on her next question, "Why have you made repeated calls to Aaron's number from your personal phone? Call history dates back to almost a couple of weeks, although she didn't have a reason to either call Aaron back then, and that too from her personal phone, or actually even have Aaron's number!"

Rachna added sarcastically as an afterthought, "The next time you plan to do something so stupid, make sure your phone is password protected. At least you won't get caught so easily."

"Sir gave me Aaron's number to follow up with him for franchising," Zeenat spoke defensively.

"No, Zeenat. I didn't give you Aaron's number," I took a chance, unsure of whether I had given the number or not.

"Then maybe Rajesh must have given the number to me, to follow up with him," hesitatingly stated Zeenat, looking at a baffled Rajesh. Rajesh was so spellbound by the attention shifting to him that he couldn't even respond to Zeenat.

"Zeenat, don't give me bull shit. Speak the truth or else I will have to call the police, and trust me, I'll ensure that they get the truth out of you," I bluffed with a high degree of assertiveness. Zeenat was an insecure person, who I knew would cave under the pressure and the thought of going to police finally collapsed her.

"I am very sorry I cheated you sir, but I promise you it'll not happen again," was her excuse for her felony.

"Why did you do it, Zeenat?" asked Anagha, "We have always treated you like family and this is how you behave."

I added, "We have taught you. We trained you to excel. And you betrayed us?"

Anagha exclaimed, "You didn't have marketing exposure, but we took the effort to train you for that! All this so that you could make extra income in your spare time in the office."

"Ma'am, Aaron offered me double the incentive for passing the leads to him. I am sorry. I made a mistake. I got lured in with greed," Zeenat was crying, uttering words amidst her sobs.

"And for a little extra money you deceived us?" I asked.

"But isn't it weird Zeenat, that you chose Aaron to pass the leads to? I mean, how did you associate with him in the first place?" inquired Rachna in a stern voice, ruthlessly interrupting Zeenat's sobs. I had started wondering that as well, but it appeared that Rachna had rehearsed the entire drama well and therefore, she was quicker with her question.

Zeenat replied, "Ever since I got Aaron's number I started contacting him. I asked him if he would pay me a commission on the short listed leads that I passed onto him. He agreed and I gave him the number of the clients who had finalized with us."

"Yes," admitted Aaron in a soft, apologetic tone, "I followed up with the leads I received from Zeenat. Mr. Prasad and Mr. Kamthe were both very happy with the designs and drawings finalized with you, so the moment I offered a cheaper price, the agreed to finalize the contract with me."

"Two clients Aaron, or three? I think you also received 'the data' of a third client, whom you've already met," Rachna suggested, albeit suspiciously.

"Yes I admit, I also received the contact of Tania Raghunathan," he spoke with guilt.

"Don't you think that you guys were just getting bolder day by day? Overconfidence trapped you this time," Rachna smiled.

"And you still had the nerve to approach me for the franchise?" I asked shocked at the revelation.

"I approached Rajesh to introduce me to you for the franchise before meeting Zeenat. I thought by the time sufficient work starts flowing in from Aurangabad, I'll do a few sites in Pune. Once I am settled there, then I'll phase out the Pune work slowly. I didn't expect you to find out about it," concluded Aaron as he rose from the seat, leaving aside the franchise agreement he was supposed to sign.

"You are disgusting, Aaron. I would love to sue you but it'll only lead to being associated with you longer. Get the bloody hell out of my office," I yelled in anger, trying to control my rage.

"Hold on,Aaron! There is one more angle to the story. I noticed a common element in all the enquiries that were forwarded to you. At first I was puzzled by it, but once the facts unveiled themselves, the jigsaw puzzle just completed itself automatically. If your sole purpose was to make money out of this then why did you only get leads of the clients that I handled? Why weren't you given the leads of clients handled by ma'am or sir?" Rachna asked with a raised eyebrow. The crafty smile was back on her face. "I think a bigger conspiracy was planned and frankly Aaron,you neither have the brain nor the guts to mastermind it. Would you do the honors of revealing his name or should I expose him myself?" was the concluding question as her eyes turned to the premier franchisee of Dessign7. "Rajesh, would you like to add to the story."

"What? Me?" Rajesh was jolted again. It was the second time that evening the focus had turned to Rajesh. "Rachna, I know you not like me but not good to blame me for your mistake."

"Rajesh, you masterminded this plan to not only weaken my credentials in this company, but also to pave your way back as marketing head in the office. Rajesh, you are neither smart nor lucky. In fact, selfish, overconfident bastards like you are seldom smart or lucky." Rachna addressed me, "Sir, Rajesh teamed up with Zeenat to get the clients' numbers. He offered her double the incentive that we were paying her to buy her loyalty. This greedy bitch got her incentive from us and then she got additional incentive from Rajesh for the same client. She forwarded only specific client numbers to him - the clients that were dealt by me. As a part of the franchise agreement, we had already shared our quotations with him for transparency. So he was well aware of the rates we would have quoted and knew exactly how much discount to offer to the clients. The sly bastard also knew that he'll require an accomplice with him, for two reasons. Firstly, being an ill-bred, crudely cultured and coarse designer, no client would prefer interacting with him directly. It would be impossible for them to trust him with the designing of their dream home. Secondly, incase a client refused to deal with this pig, and decided to inform us of his lecherous proposal, then at least he would be able to save his pretentious face with you, the back stabbing bastard!" she pointed to Rajesh and yelled. "Aaron interacted with clients, maintaining himself as the face of the organization. We didn't know him or his firm, 'AJ & Associates'. He got his share of professional fees. Zeenat passed the leads and she got her share of the money. The mastermind, venomous viper of this operation was Rajesh,who got the contract of the entire project, making illegitimate money at the expense of his mentors.

"But that is not all that the bastard was aiming for. Rajesh knew if he moved fast, we'd be onto him. He had to keep it slow. He couldn't steal all our clients - he would be trapped immediately - so he told Zeenat to only pass leads of the client that I had met," Rachna spoke in a disgusted tone. "He knew that I was fresh with marketing and my sales pitch could easily be accepted as weak, hence the client was lost. Secondly, he could also undermine my confidence and my reputation, by proving my incapability to handle all aspects of the company independently."

"Good story madam," clapped Rajesh sarcastically, but before he could speak further, Rachna shut him up. She held out her phone with a photograph from earlier that morning, showing Aaron accompanied by Rajesh entering Mr. Prasad's site.

"Actually that's how I recognized Aaron."

As the photograph flashed on the screen, I looked at Rajesh questioningly for an explanation. Rajesh was frozen, even his stammering words refused to be spoken. The cabin had shrunk to an awkward size, where Anagha, Rachna and I were suffocating because of the malice present in the room. Abuses were hurled at the three leeches, who tried to the suck life out of the very organization that hosted them. I exercised a lot of self-control to prevent myself from throwing a few punches. Our culprits stood silently in front of us like satanic statues, remorsefully awaiting the end of their torment. They had run out excuses to justify their selfish acts, and we had exhausted our vocabulary of abuses. The deceit around me had sapped my energy. I stood still in disbelief. An era of silence followed. There were six pairs of tearful eyes in the room, questioningly staring at each other.

Aaron, who was the least of our culprits and who didn't even matter now, had tears of shame. He never imagined that he would ever be invited to a party to be abused so harshly. He wept, as he slowly moved out of the room, regretting Rajesh's alliance.

Zeenat's tears had a selfish regret. She was sobbing because she received her pink slip then and there. She wasn't ashamed of her deed. She just didn't want to lose her job. Her financial instability would not permit her to lose this job. She had to support her family. Although she begged for her job, we did not sympathize with her. She too crept her way out of the office, after we confiscated her official mobile phone and deleted all the official contacts from her personal phone.

An earlier incident of fraud was already to Rajesh's credit, which I had generously forgotten, owing to my affection for him. And it was because of this affection that I finally spoke to him, "Rajesh, three years ago when you cheated me, I consoled myself thinking that you did it out of financial pressures. So, when you came back, I believed that you must have changed with time, now that you were well off. I assumed that your regret and loyalty were genuine when you consistently wished me on all occasions, every year.

"Previously, when you deceived me, you took projects which you knew I would refuse. At least you were not harming the company. But this time you started stealing from our company itself. It had laid the foundation for your distinguished career. This is truly parasitic." I recalled

Rajesh's words and repeated them, "Trust me! This is what you had asked me – to trust you. And I always did trust you. But, today my faith is shattered. I always had a lot of genuine care and affection for you. I only wish you could appreciate it."

Anagha and Rachna, well aware of this affection, were angry for the pain that Rajesh had caused me. The business loss was secondary to them. They had tears in their eyes knowing that I was hurt. As for Rajesh, he was left with no option but to silently burn in the hell he had just created for himself. He was abused in the foulest of all languages; he was tormented with treacherous titles; he was insulted in front of his accomplices and he lost credit with his mentors. He had just cut his golden goose and that regret cocktailed with humiliation and infamy, rolled down as tears from his eyes.

Before Rajesh was finally thrown out the office, I expressed my final realization to him, "I always regarded you as a pillar of support but I neglected the fact that ambition can destroy the foundation of any pillar."

***

I too had tears in my eyes. I was disgusted with the deception. Rajesh, who was the godfather of the company had stolen from his own child. But later when I looked back, I also had a sparkle of joy within me. I could see before me, Rachna, fighting loyally for me, ready to defend me against the likes of a hundred Rajesh. It was not only her loyalty, but also her ability to shield Dessign7, that overwhelmed me. She had evolved completely like the butterfly. She was soaring high in the sky. In fact higher than I had expected her to. And I was proud of her. She could protect the company and aggressively drive it forward to greater statures. She was my weapon; she was my shield, this was her blessing, this was her curse.

16 End it Again

The next morning, as I walked into the office, I was greeted with positive laughter from the two ladies waiting at the reception. I knew Rachna, but I could barely recollect the other face. It was familiar yet out of context. After straining my grey cells, I remembered her as Tania, the client whom Rachna had met a week ago. For a fraction of a second, I looked at the reception table, expecting my usual 'Good Morning, Sir' from Zeenat, but then remembered the office clean-up that we conducted the previous evening. Zeenat and Rajesh were out of Dessign7 on account of betrayal. As I walked past the reception and entered my cabin, I flashed a smile to Tania and I requested, "Rachna, come in please."

Rachna followed me into the cabin with Tania. As we all took our seats, Rachna introduced us, "This is Tania Raghunathan, my friend, and this is Shabbir Sabuwala, the director of Dessign7." Slightly taken aback by the introduction, I shook hands with Tania. I was expecting her to be introduced as a client rather than a friend. Rachna began her narration, "After we lost two clients, I had a hunch that client information was being leaked out of office. Otherwise never before had we lost out on a finalized client. I had an instinct that something fishy was going on, but didn't know whom to doubt. So, I thought the best way to trace the culprit in the chain of events was to start from the top." I heard the narration with keen interest.

Rachna continued "I sought help of Tania, my college friend. I asked her to call the office number and pose as a client who has a 2 BHK at B.T. Kawade Road. Zeenat passed the inquiry to you but I obviously handled the client since it was my reference. Tania came for a meeting to office as planned. Zeenat ensured that the meeting was well conducted. I presented the entire proposal to Tania, like we would do to any other client. She concluded the meeting, assuring to revert the following afternoon. I updated Zeenat about her feedback, and before Tania could revert, she received a call from someone called Aaron James requesting a meeting. Tania messaged the gist of the conversation to me. At that point in time, I figured that Zeenat and Aaron were allied, but I didn't understand the source of that alliance. I didn't understand how Zeenat knew Aaron so well that she'd pass client information to him. I requested Tania to meet Aaronand she agreed to do so. She met Aaron at her residence, and the meeting was attended by two gentlemen. One was Aaron and the other was introduced as Rajesh, his partner. Aaron presented the AJ & Associates' company profile and Rajesh handled all the technical queries raised by Tania. Both of them assured Tania that the work quality would be as premium as Dessign7's work, at a much cheaper cost due to lesser overhead expenses. Tania concluded their meeting with an assurance to revert to them. She immediately informed me of all the details. I knew Aaron was coming to sign the franchise agreement, so I asked Tania to convey a week's delay in her decision and she asked Aaron to call her after a week. Unsuspecting that I was aware of their scheme, the trio assembled in office to sign up Aaronas a franchisee. The rest you know."

Throughout the narration, Tania and I were quiet. I was grasping the situation being related to me, whereas Tania, like a good friend, was allowing Rachna to bask in the limelight. I was still recovering from the revelation and was little lost when I finally spoke, "Wow! You actually orchestrated the entire plan to corner these guys. I am impressed." Extending a handshake to Tania, I spoke, "Thanks a lot Tania, not only have you done a lot for your friend, but have also done a huge favor to the company. If it wasn't for your support, I don't know how much more we would have lost. You realize, of course, that I am quite short of words. But thanks a lot for your support. If there is any help that I can extend at any time, please feel free to ask."

Tania humbly extended courtesy, "The pleasure was mine. I enjoyed playing the detective. The suspense, the thrill, the scheme, the plan; it was all worth it." Then looking towards Rachna she made a final statement, "It was for a friend, a very good friend!"

Tania and I exchanged goodbyes. The two ladies stood up to leave the cabin.

***

I looked at the two ladies leave the cabin, as they slowly allowed the frosted glass door to close behind them. I looked around the cabin, a little lost, recalling yesterday's incident. I could visualize the images of a cabin full of people hurling abuses and shedding tears. They were known faces of people I loved and cared for, but they were distressed.

I snapped back to the reality of the empty room which I solely occupied. I glanced to the wall on my left which displayed my certificates and photographs. I noticed one of the frames in particular and although I had written the poem myself, I felt like reading it again today. The title read "My First Earning". It was a gift that I had given to Anagha, my wife, a couple of years ago on her birthday. My focus shifted for a couple of seconds as I heard a giggle outside the cabin and I saw a hazy silhouette of one of the ladies leave the office. I continued to read my poem framed on the wall:

"With every growth, and every milestone,
With every obstacle that you cross,
Remember the spark that ignited the fire,
Always remember the very first.

Look forward to achieve greater tasks
March ahead to amass more and more,
But once a while, reflect on the past,
To take a look at your very first."

The words "Remember the spark that ignited the fire" haunted me, especially in context with yesterday's event. I journeyed deep into the past to remember the spark that ignited the fire, but ventured a little too deep into the past.

Suddenly, a car with a blaring horn, passing by below the office disturbed my flashback. As I looked around the room again, I remembered that there was an important errand for the day. I dialed the extension number 305 and spoke, "Rachna, can you come in please?"

"Please give me five minutes sir, I will finish the work on hand and be there," she replied. Rachna's request got me a few more minutes to continue my remembrance of yesteryears.

Rachna entered the cabin a few minutes later. As she sat across the table, I congratulated her on the crackdown of the conspiracy. I turned around, opened the drawer, and removed the locked away document which Rachna truly deserved. "Today you have once again proved that you truly deserve this," I spoke as I handed over the "Certificate of Appreciation".

Rachna accepted the certificate, her smile reflecting her pride on not only defending her position in the firm, but more importantly defending the firm itself.

She walked out of the cabin, leaving me proud of her. I promised myself that someday I'll write a book to tell the world of how a young girl who entered our office as an intern grew to be such a pillar of support. And when I do write the book, I shall aptly call it "The Growing Years".

17 The Growing Years

Although an incident in the life of Dessign7 Interiors Pvt. Ltd. ended, the firm itself still continues to thrive. That incident made all of us a lot stronger and we went on to build a stronger network of franchisees. Dessign7 Interiors Pvt. Ltd. still strives to become the premier choice of anyone willing to do interior designing for their residence, under the able guidance of Anagha, Rachna and myself.

Zeenat is still looking for a job and calls me up once a while asking for forgiveness. Rajesh never called after that but I always wish him luck to succeed in any venture he does. Aaron finally settled in Aurangabad with his family business of electronic store. Vaishali is happy that, although she had considered Rajesh's offer, she never accepted it. She is hoping that someday she will become a pillar of support.

Dessign7 Interiors Pvt. Ltd., Rachna, Anagha and I are still growing with every passing year, as we still refer to our time as "The Growing Years".